The Solitude of Compassion

The Solitude of Compassion

Jean Giono

TRANSLATED BY EDWARD FORD

SEVEN STORIES PRESS
New York | Toronto | London | Sydney

Seven Stories Press
140 Watts Street
New York NY 10013
http://www.sevenstories.com

In Canada: Hushion House, 36 Northline Road, Toronto, Ontario M4B 3E2

In the U.K.: Turnaround Publisher Services Ltd., Unit 3, Olympia Trading Estate, Coburg Road, Wood Green, London N22 6TZ

In Australia: Tower Books, 2/17 Rodborough Road, Frenchs Forest NSW 2086

Library of Congress Cataloging-in-Publication Data

Giono, Jean, 1895–1970.
[Solitude de la pitié. English]
The solitude of compassion / Jean Giono; translated by Edward Ford.
    p.   cm,
ISBN 1-58322-524-2
1. Ford, Edward (Edward Bruce) II. Title.
PQ2613.I57 S613 2002
843'.912—dc21   2002010009

9 8 7 6 5 4 3 2 1

College professors may order examination copies of Seven Stories Press titles for a free six-month trial period. To order, visit www.sevenstories.com/textbook, or fax on school letterhead to (212) 226-1411.

Book design by JG

Printed in Canada

Contents

Foreword: From "The Books in My Life"
by Henry Miller   7
The Solitude of Compassion   35
Prelude to Pan   45
Fields   67
Ivan Ivanovitch Kossiakoff   79
The Hand   95
Annette or a Family Affair   99
On the Side of the Road   103
Jofroi de Maussan   107
Philémon   121
Joselet   127
Sylvie   133
Babeau   137
The Sheep   141
In the Land of the Tree Cutters   145
The Big Fence   149
Destruction of Paris   153
Magnetism   157
Fear of the Land   161
Lost Rafts   165
Song of the World   169

5

from "The Books in My Life" by Henry Miller

It was in the rue d'Alésia, in one of those humble stationery stores which sell books, that I first came across Jean Giono's works. It was the daughter of the proprietor—bless her soul!—who literally thrust upon me the book called *Que ma joie demeure!* (*The Joy of Man's Desiring*). In 1939, after making a pilgrimage to Manosque with Giono's boyhood friend, Henri Fluchère, the latter bought for me *Jean le Bleu* (*Blue Boy*), which I read on the boat going to Greece. Both these French editions I lost in my wanderings. On returning to America, however, I soon made the acquaintance of Pascal Covici, one of the editors of the Viking Press, and through him I got acquainted with all that has been translated of Giono—not very much, I sadly confess.

Between times I have maintained a random correspondence with Giono, who continues to live in the place of his birth, Manosque. How often I have regretted that I did not meet him on the occasion of my visit to his home—he was off then on a walking expedition through the countryside he describes with such deep poetic imagination in his books. But if I never meet him in the flesh I can certainly say that I have met him in the spirit. And so have many others throughout this wide world. Some, I find, know him only through the screen versions of his books—*Harvest* and *The Baker's Wife*. No one ever leaves the theatre, after a performance of these films, with a dry eye. No one ever looks upon a loaf of bread, after seeing *Harvest*, in quite the same way as he used to; nor, after seeing *The Baker's Wife*, does one think of the cuckold with the same raucous levity.

But these are trifling observations...

A few moments ago, tenderly flipping the pages of his books, I was saying to myself: "Tenderize your finger tips! Make yourself ready for the great task!"

For several years now I have been preaching the gospel—of Jean Giono. I do not say that my words have fallen upon deaf ears, I merely complain that my audience has been restricted. I do not doubt that I have made myself a nuisance at the Viking Press in New York, for I keep pestering them intermittently to speed up the translations of Giono's works. Fortunately I am able to read Giono in his own tongue and, at the risk of sounding immodest, *in his own idiom*. But, as ever, I continue to think of the countless thousands in England and America who must wait until his books are translated. I feel that I could convert to the ranks of his ever-growing admirers innumerable readers whom his American publishers despair of reaching. I think I could even sway the hearts of those who have never heard of him—in England, Australia, New Zealand and other places where the English language is spoken. But I seem incapable of moving those few pivotal beings who hold, in a manner of speaking, his destiny in their hands. Neither with logic nor passion, neither with statistics nor examples, can I budge the position of editors and publishers in this, my native land. I shall probably succeed in getting Giono translated into Arabic, Turkish and Chinese before I convince his American publishers to go forward with the task they so sincerely began.

Flipping the pages of *The Joy of Man's Desiring*—I was looking for the reference to Orion "looking like Queen Anne's lace"—I noticed these words of Bobi, the chief figure in the book:

> I have never been able to show people things. It's curious. I have always been reproached for it. They say: 'No one sees what you mean.'

Nothing could better express the way I feel at times. Hesitatingly I add—Giono, too, must often experience this sense of frustration. Otherwise I am unable to account for the fact that, despite the incontrovertible logic of dollars and cents with which his publishers always silence me, his works have not spread like wildfire on this continent.

I am never convinced by the sort of logic referred to. I may be silenced, but I am not convinced. On the other hand, I must confess that I do not know the formula for "success," as publishers use the term. I doubt if they do either. Nor do I think a man like Giono would thank me for making him a commercial success. He would like to be read more, certainly. What author does not? Like every author, he would especially like to be read by those who see what he means.

Herbert Read paid him a high tribute in a paper written during the War. He referred to him as the "peasant-anarchist." (I am sure his publishers are not keen to advertise such a label!) I do not think of Giono, myself, either as peasant or anarchist, though I regard neither term as pejorative. (Neither does Herbert Read, to be sure.) If Giono is an anarchist, then so were Emerson and Thoreau. If Giono is a peasant, then so was Tolstoy. But we do not begin to touch the essence of these great figures in regarding them from these aspects, these angles. Giono ennobles the peasant in his narratives; Giono enlarges the concept of anarchism in his philosophic adumbrations. When he touches a man like our own Herman Melville, in the book called *Pour Saluer Melville* (which the Viking Press refuses to bring our, though it was translated for them), we come very close to the real Giono—and, what is even more important, close to the real Melville. This Giono is a poet. His poetry is of the imagination and reveals itself just as forcibly in his prose. It is through this function that Giono reveals his power to captivate men and women everywhere, regardless of rank, class, status or pursuit. This is the legacy left him by his parents, particularly, I feel, by his father, of whom he has written so tenderly, so movingly, in *Blue Boy*. In his Corsican blood there is a strain which, like the wines of Greece when added to French vintages, lend body and tang to the Gallic tongue. As for the soil in which he is rooted, and for which his true patriotism never fails to manifest itself, only a wizard, it seems to me, could relate cause to effect. Like our own Faulkner, Giono has created his own private terrestrial domain, a mythical domain far closer to reality than books of history or geography. It is a region over which the stars and planets course with throbbing pulsations. It is a land in which things "happen" to men as aeons ago they happened to the gods. Pan still walks the earth. The soil is saturated with cosmic juices. Events "transpire." Miracles occur. And never does the author betray the figures, the characters, whom he has conjured out of the womb of his rich imagination. His men and women have their prototypes in the legends of provincial

France, in the songs of the troubadors, in the daily doings of humble, unknown peasants, an endless line of them, from Charlemagne's day to the very present. In Giono's works we have the sombreness of Hardy's moors, the eloquence of Lawrence's flowers and lowly creatures, the enchantment and sorcery of Arthur Machen's Welsh settings, the freedom and violence of Faulkner's world, the buffoonery and licence of the medieval mystery plays. And with all this a pagan charm and sensuality which stems from the ancient Greek world.

If we look back on the ten years preceding the outbreak of the war, the years of steep incline into disaster, then the significant figures in the French scene are not the Gides and the Valérys, or any competitor for the laurels of the Académie, but Giono, the peasant-anarchist, Bernanos, the integral Christian, and Bréton, the super-realist. These are the significant figures, and they are positive figures, creative because destructive, moral in their revolt against contemporary values. Apparently they are disparate figures, working in different spheres, along different levels of human consciousness; but in the total sphere of that consciousness their orbits meet, and include within their points of contact nothing that is compromising, reactionary or decadent; but contain everything that is positive, revolutionary, and creative of a new and enduring world.[1]

Giono's revolt against contemporary values runs through all his books. In *Refusal to Obey*, which appeared in translation only in James Cooney's little magazine, *The Phoenix*, so far as I know,

Giono spoke out manfully against war, against conscription, against bearing arms. Such diatribes do not help to make an author more popular in his native land. When the next war comes such a man is marked: whatever he says or does is reported in the papers, exaggerated, distorted, falsified. The men who have their country's interest most at heart are the very ones to be vilified, to be called "traitors," "renegades" or worse. Here is an impassioned utterance made by Giono in *Blue Boy*. It may throw a little light on the nature of his revolt. It begins:

I don't remember how my friendship for Louis David began. At this moment, as I speak of him, I can no longer recall my pure youth, the enchantment of the magicians and of the days. I am steeped in blood. Beyond this book there is a deep wound from which all men of my age are suffering. This side of the page is soiled with pus and darkness…

If you (Louis) had only died for honorable things; if you had fought for love or in getting food for your little ones. But, no. First they deceived you and then they killed you in the war.

What do you want me to do with this France that you have helped, it seems, to preserve, as I too have done? What shall we do with it, we who have lost all our friends? Ah! If it were a question of defending rivers, hills, mountains, skies, winds, rains, I would say, 'Willingly. That is our job. Let us fight. All our happiness in life is there.' No, we have defended the sham name of all that. When I see a river, I say 'river'; when I see a tree, I say 'tree'; I never say 'France.' That does not exist.

Ah! How willingly would I give away that false name that one single one of those dead, the simplest, the most humble, might live again! Nothing can be put into the scales with the human heart. They are all the time talking about God! It is God who gave the tiny shove with His finger to the pendulum of the clock of blood at the instant the child dropped from its mother's womb. They are always talking about God, when the only product of His good workmanship, the only thing that is godlike, the life that He alone can create, in spite of all your science of bespectacled idiots, that life you destroy at will in an infamous mortar of slime and spit, with the blessing of all your churches. What logic!

There is no glory in being French. There is only one glory: in being alive.

When I read a passage like this I am inclined to make extravagant statements. Somewhere I believe I said that if I had to choose between France and Giono I would choose Giono. I have the same feeling about Whitman. For me Walt Whitman is a hundred, a thousand, times more *America* than America itself. It was the great Democrat himself who wrote thus about our vaunted democracy:

We have frequently printed the word Democracy. Yet I cannot too often repeat that it is a word the real gist of which still sleeps, quite unawakened, notwithstanding the resonance and the many angry tempests out of which its syllables have come, from pen and tongue. It is a great word, whose history, I suppose, remains unwritten, because that history has yet to be enacted.[2]

No, a man like Giono could never be a traitor, not even if he folded his hands and allowed the enemy to overrun his country. In *Maurizius Forever*, wherein I devoted some pages to his *Refusal to Obey*, I put it thus, and I repeat it with even greater vehemence: "I say there is something wrong with a society which, because it quarrels with a man's views, can condemn him as an arch-enemy. Giono is not a traitor. Society is the traitor. Society is a traitor to its fine principles, its empty principles. Society is constantly looking for victims—and finds them among the glorious in spirit."

What was it Goethe said to Eckermann? Interesting indeed that the "first European" should have expressed himself thus: "Men will become more clever and more acute; but not better, happier, and stronger in action—or at least only at epochs. I foresee the time when God will break up everything for a renewed creation. I am certain that everything is planned to this end, and that the time and hour in the distant future for occurrence of this renovating epoch are already fixed…"

The other day someone mentioned in my presence how curious and repetitive was the rôle of the father in authors' lives. We had been speaking of Joyce, of Utrillo, of Thomas Wolfe, of Lawrence, of Céline, of Van Gogh, of Cendrars, and then of Egyptian myths and of the legends of Crete. We spoke of those who had never found their father, of those who were forever seeking a father. We spoke of Joseph and his brethren, of Jonathan and David, of the magic connected with names such as the Hellespont and Fort Ticonderoga. As they spoke I was frantically searching my memory for instances where the mother played a great rôle. I could think only of two, but they were truly illustrious names—Goethe and da Vinci. Then I began to speak of *Blue Boy*. I looked for the extraordinary passage, so meaningful to a writer, wherein Giono tells what his father meant to him.

> If I have such love for the memory of my father, it begins, if I can never separate myself from his image, if time cannot cut the thread, it is because in the experience of every single day I realize all that he has done for me. He was the first to recognize my sensuousness. He was the first to see, with his gray eyes, that sensuousness that made me touch a wall and imagine the roughness like porous skin. That sensuousness that prevented me from learning music, putting a higher price on the intoxication of listening than on the joy of being skillful, that sensuousness that made me like a drop of water pierced by the sun, pierced by the shapes and colors in the world, bearing in truth, like a drop of water, the form, the color, the sound, the sensation, physically in my flesh...
> He broke nothing, tore nothing in me, stifled nothing, effaced nothing with his moistened finger. With the prescience of an insect he gave the remedies to the little larva that I was: one day this, the next day that; he weighted me with plants, trees, earth, men, hills, women, grief, goodness, pride, all these as remedies, all these as provision, in prevision of what might be a running sore, but which, thanks to him, became an immense sun within me.

Towards the close of the book, the father nearing his end, they have a quiet talk under a linden tree. "Where I made a mistake," says his father, "was when I wanted to be good and helpful. You will make a mistake, like me."

Heart-rending words. Too true, too true. I wept when I read this. I weep again in recalling his father's words. I weep for Giono, for myself, for all who have striven to be "good and helpful." For those who are still striving, even though they know in their hearts that it is a "mistake." What we know is nothing compared to what we feel impelled to do out of the goodness of our hearts. Wisdom can never be transmitted from one to another. And in the ultimate do we not abandon wisdom for love?

There is another passage in which father and son converse with Franchese Odripano. They had been talking about the art of healing.

'When a person has a pure breath,' my father said, 'he can put out wounds all about him like so many lamps.'

But I was not so sure. I said, 'If you put out all the lamps, Papa, you won't be able to see any more.'

At that moment the velvet eyes were still and they were looking beyond my glorious youth.

That is true,' he replied, 'the wounds illumine. That is true. You listen to Odripano a good deal. He has had experience. If he can stay young amongst us it is because he is a poet. Do you know what poetry is? Do you know that what he says is poetry? Do you know that, son? It is essential to realize that. Now listen. I, too, have had my experiences, and I tell you that you must put out the wounds. If, when you get to be a man, you know these two things, poetry and the science of extinguishing wounds, then you *will* be a man.'

I beg the reader's indulgence for quoting at such length from Giono's works. If I thought for one moment that most everyone was familiar with Giono's writings I would indeed be embarrassed to have made these citations. A friend of mine said the other day that practically everyone he had met knew Jean Giono. "You mean his books?" I asked. "At least some of them," he said. "At any rate, they certainly know what he stands for." "That's another story," I replied. "You're lucky to move in such circles. I have quite another story to tell about Giono. I doubt sometimes that even his editors have read him. *How to read*, that's the question."

That evening, glancing through a book by Holbrook Jackson,[3] I stumbled on Coleridge's four classes of readers. Let me cite them:

1. Sponges, who absorb all they read, and return it nearly in the same state, only a little dirtied.
2. Sand-glasses, who retain nothing, and are content to get through a book for the sake of getting through the time.
3. Strain-bags, who retain merely the dregs of what they read.
4. Mogul diamonds, equally rare and valuable, who profit by what they read, and enable others to profit by it also.

Most of us belong in the third category, if not also in one of the first two. Rare indeed are the mogul diamonds! And now I wish to make an observation connected with the lending of Giono's books. The few I possess—among them *The Song of the World* and *Lovers are never Losers*, which I see I have not mentioned—have been loaned over and over again to all who expressed a desire to become acquainted with Jean Giono. This means that I have not only handed them to a considerable number of visitors but that I have wrapped and mailed the books to numerous others, to some in foreign lands as well. To no author I have recommended has there been a response such as hailed the reading of Giono. The reactions have been virtually unanimous. "Magnificent! Thank you, thank you!" that is the usual return. Only one person disapproved, said flatly that he could make nothing of Giono, and that was a man dying of cancer. I had lent him *The Joy of Man's Desiring*. He was one of those "successful" business men who had achieved everything and found nothing to sustain him. I think we may regard his verdict as exceptional. The others, and they include men and women of all ages, all walks of life, men and women of the most diverse views, the most conflicting aims and tendencies, all proclaimed their love, admiration and gratitude for Jean Giono. They do not represent a "select" audience, they were chosen at random. The one qualification which they had in common was a thirst for good books...

These are my private statistics, which I maintain are as valid as the publisher's. It is the hungry and thirsty who will eventually decide the future of Giono's works.

There is another man, a tragic figure, whose book I often thrust upon friends and acquaintances: Vaslav Nijinsky. His *Diary* is in some strange way connected with *Blue Boy*. It tells me something about writing. It is the writing of a man who is part lucid, part mad. It is a communication so naked, so desperate, that it breaks the mold. We are face to face with reality, and it is almost unbearable. The technique, so utterly personal, is one from which every writer can learn. Had he not gone to the asylum, had this been merely his baptismal work, we would have had in Nijinsky a writer equal to the dancer.

I mention this book because I have scanned it closely. Though it may sound presumptuous to say so, it is a book for writers. I cannot limit Giono in this way, but I must say that he, too, feeds the writer, instructs the writer, inspires the writer. In *Blue Boy* he gives us the genesis of a writer, telling it with the consummate art of a practiced writer. One feels that he is a "born writer." One feels that he might also be a painter, a musician (despite what he says). It is the "Storyteller's Story," *l'histoire de l'histoire*. It peels away the wrappings in which we mummify writers and reveals the embryonic being. It gives us the physiology, the chemistry, the physics, the biology of that curious animal, the writer. It is a textbook dipped in the magic fluid of the medium it expounds. It connects us with the source of all creative activity. It breathes, it palpitates, it renews the blood stream. It is the kind of book which every man who thinks he has at least one story to tell could write but which he never does, alas. It is the story which authors are telling over and over again in myriad disguises. Seldom does it come straight from the delivery room. Usually it is washed and dressed first. Usually it is given a name which is not the true name.

His sensuousness, the development of which Giono attributes to his father's delicate nurturing, is without question one of the cardinal features of his art. It invests his characters, his landscapes, his whole narrative. "Let us refine our finger tips, our points of contact with the world…" Giono has done just this. The result is that we detect in his music the use of an instrument which has undergone the same ripening process as the player. In Giono the music and the instrument are one. That is his special gift. If he did not become a musician because, as he says, he thought it more important to be a good listener, he has become a writer who has raised listening to such an art that we follow his melodies as if we had written them ourselves. We no longer know, in reading his books, whether we are listening to Giono or to ourselves. We are not even aware that we are listening. We live through his words and in them, as naturally as if we were respiring at a comfortable altitude or floating on the bosom of the deep or swooping like a hawk with the down-draught of a canyon. The actions of his narratives are cushioned in this terrestrial effluvium; the machinery never grinds because it is perpetually laved by cosmic lubricants. Giono gives us men, beasts and gods—in their *molecular* constituency.[4] He has seen no need to descend to the atomic arena. He deals in galaxies and constellations, in troupes, herds, and flocks, in biological plasm as well as primal magma and plasma. The names of his characters, as well as the hills and streams which surround them, have the tang, the aroma, the vigor and the spice of strong herbs. They are autochthonous names, redolent of the Midi. When we pronounce them we revive the memory of other times; unknowingly we inhale a whiff of the African shore. We suspect that Atlantis was not so distant either in time or space.

It is a little over twenty years now since Giono's *Colline*, published in translation as *Hill of Destiny*, by Brentano's, New York, made the author known at once throughout the reading world. In his introduction to the American edition, Jacques le Clercq, the translator, explains the purpose of the *Prix Brentano*, which was first awarded to Jean Giono.

> For the French public, the *Prix Brentano* owes its importance to various novel features. To begin with, it is the first American Foundation to crown a French work and to insure the publication of that work in America. The mere fact that it comes from abroad—*"l'étranger, cette postérité contemporaine"*—arouses a lively interest; again, the fact that the jury was composed of foreigners gave ample assurance that there could be no *propagande de chapelle* here, no manoeuvres of cliques such as must nec-

essarily attend French prize-awards. Finally the material value of the prize itself proved of good augur.

Twenty years since! And just a few months ago I received two new books from Giono—*Un Roi Sans Divertissement* and *Noé*—the first two of a series of twenty. A series of *"Chroniques,"* he calls them. He was thirty years old when *Colline* won the *Prix Brentano*. In the interval he has written a respectable number of books. And now, in his fifties, he has projected a series of twenty, of which several have already been written. Just before the war started he had begun his celebrated translation of *Moby Dick*, a labor of several years, in which he was aided by two capable women whose names are given along with his as translators of the book. An immense undertaking, since Giono is not fluent in English. But, as he explains in the book which followed—*Pour Saluer Melville*—*Moby Dick* was his constant companion for years during his walks over the hills. He had lived with the book and it had become a part of him. It was inevitable that he should be the one to make it known to the French public. I have read parts of this translation and it seems to me an inspired one. Melville is not one of my favorites. *Moby Dick* has always been a sort of *bête noir* for me. But in reading the French version, which I prefer to the original, I have come to the conclusion that I will some day read the book. After reading *Pour Saluer Melville*, which is a poet's interpretation of a poet—"a pure invention," as Giono himself says in a letter—I was literally beside myself. How often it is the "foreigner" who teaches us to appreciate our own authors! (I think immediately of that wonderful study of Walt Whitman by a Frenchman who virtually dedicated his life to the subject. I think, too, of what Baudelaire did to make Poe's name a by-word throughout all Europe.) Over and over again we see that the understanding of a language is not the same as the understanding of language. It is always communion versus communication. Even in translation some of us understand Dostoievsky, for example, better than his Russian contemporaries—or, shall I say, better than our present Russian contemporaries.

I noticed, in reading the Introduction to *Hill of Destiny*, that the translator expressed apprehension that the book might offend certain "squeamish" American readers. It is curious how askance French authors are regarded by Anglo-Saxons. Even some of the good Catholic writers of France are looked upon as "immoral." It always reminds me of my father's anger when he caught me reading *The Wild Ass' Skin*. All he needed was to see the name Balzac. That was enough to convince him that the book was "immoral." (Fortunately he never caught me reading *Droll Stories!*) My father, of course, had never read a line of Balzac. He had hardly read a line of any English or American author, indeed. The one writer he confessed to reading—*c'est inoui, mais c'est vrai!*—was John Ruskin. *Ruskin!* I nearly fell off the chair when he blurted this out. I did not know how to account for such an absurdity, but later I discovered that it was the minister who had (temporarily) converted him to Christ who was responsible. What astounded me even more was his admission that he had enjoyed reading Ruskin. That still remains inexplicable to me. But of Ruskin another time...

In Giono's books, as in Cendrars' and so many, many French books, there are always wonderful accounts of eating and drinking. Sometimes it is a feast, as in *The Joy of Man's Desiring*, sometimes it is a simple repast. Whatever it be, it makes one's mouth water. (There still remains to be written, by an American for Americans, a cookbook based on the recipes gleaned from the pages of French literature.) Every cinéaste has observed the prominence given by French film directors to eating and drinking. It is a feature conspicuously absent in American movies. When we have such a scene it is seldom real, neither the food nor the participants. In France, whenever two or more come together there is sensual as well as spiritual communion. With what longing American youths look at these scenes. Often it is a repast al fresco. Then are we even more moved, for truly we know little of the joy of eating and drinking outdoors. The Frenchman "loves" his food. We take food for nourishment or because we are unable to dispense with the habit. The Frenchman, even if he is a man of the cities, is closer to the soil than the American. He does not tamper with or refine away the products of the soil. He relishes the homely meals as much as the creations of the gourmet. He likes things fresh, not canned or refrigerated. And almost every Frenchman knows how to cook. I have never met a Frenchman who did not know how to make such a simple thing as an omelette, for example. But I know plenty of Americans who cannot even boil an egg.

Naturally, with good food goes good conversation, another element completely lacking in our country. To have good conversation it is almost imperative to have good wine with the meal. Not cocktails, not whisky, not cold beer or ale. Ah, the wines! The variety of them, the subtle, indescribable effects they produce! And let me not forget that with good food goes beautiful women—women who, in addition to stimulating one's appetite, know how to inspire good conversation. How horrible are our banquets for men only! How we love to castrate, to mutilate ourselves! How we really loathe all that is sensuous and sensual! I believe most earnestly that what repels Americans more than immorality is the pleasure to be derived from the enjoyment of the five senses. We are not a "moral" people by any means. We do not need to read *La Peau* by Malaparte to discover what beasts are hidden beneath our chivalric uniforms. And when

I say "uniforms" I mean the garb which disguises the civilian as well as that which disguises the soldier. We are men in uniform through and through. We are not individuals, neither are we members of a great collectivity. We are neither democrats, communists, socialists nor anarchists. We are an unruly mob. And the sign by which we are known is vulgarity.

There is never vulgarity in even the coarsest pages of Giono. There may be lust, carnality, sensuality—but not vulgarity. His characters may indulge in sexual intercourse occasionally, they may even be said to "fornicate," but in these indulgences there is never anything horripilating as in Malaparte's descriptions of American soldiers abroad. Never is a French writer obliged to resort to the mannerisms of Lawrence in a book such as *Lady Chatterley's Lover*. Lawrence should have known Giono, with whom he has much in common, by the way. He should have travelled up from Vence to the plateau of Haute-Provence where describing the setting of *Colline*, Giono says: "an endless waste of blue earth, village after village lying in death on the lavender tableland. A handful of men, how pitifully few, how ineffectual! And, crouching amid the grasses, wallowing in the reeds—the hill, like a bull." But Lawrence was then already in the grip of death, able nevertheless to give us *The Man Who Died* or *The Escaped Cock*. Still enough breath in him, as it were, to reject the sickly Christian image of a suffering Redeemer and restore the image of man in flesh and blood, a man content just to live, just to breathe. A pity he could not have met Giono in the early days of his life. Even the boy Giono would have been able to divert him from some of his errors. Lawrence was forever railing against the French, though he enjoyed living in France, it would seem. He saw only what was sick, what was "decadent," in the French. Wherever he went he saw that first—his nose was too keen. Giono so rooted in his native soil, Lawrence so filled with wanderlust. Both proclaiming the life abundant: Giono in hymns of life, Lawrence in hymns of hate. Just as Giono has anchored himself in his "region," so has he anchored himself in the tradition of art. He has not suffered because of these restrictions, self-imposed. On the contrary, he has flowered. Lawrence jutted out of his world and out of the realm of art. He wandered over the earth like a lost soul, finding peace nowhere. He exploited the novel to preach the resurrection of man, but himself perished miserably. I owe a great debt to D. H. Lawrence. These observations and comparisons are not intended as a rejection of the man, they are offered merely as indications of his limitations. Just because I am also an Anglo-Saxon, I feel free to stress his faults. We have all of us a terrible need of France. I have said it over and over again. I shall probably do so until I die.

Vive la France! Vive Jean Giono!

It was just five months ago that I put aside these pages on Jean Giono, knowing that I had more to say but determined to hold off until the right moment came. Yesterday I had an unexpected visit from a literary agent whom I knew years ago in Paris. He is the sort of individual who on entering a house goes through your library first, fingering your books and manuscripts, before looking at you. And when he does look at you he sees not *you* but only what is exploitable in you. After remarking, rather asininely, I thought, that his one aim was to be of help to writers, I took the cue and mentioned Giono's name.

"There's a man you could do something for, if what you say is true," I said flatly. I showed him *Pour Saluer Melville*. I explained that Viking seemed to have no desire to publish any more of Giono's books.

"And do you know why?" he demanded.

I told him what they had written me.

"That's not the real reason," he replied, and proceeded to give me what he "knew" to be the real reason.

"And even if what you say is true," said I, "though I don't believe it, there remains this book which I want to see published. It is a beautiful book. I love it."

"In fact," I added, "my love and admiration for Giono is such that it doesn't matter a damn to me what he does or what he is said to have done. I know my Giono."

He looked at me quizzically and, as if to provoke me, asserted: "There are *several* Gionos, you know."

I knew what he was implying but I answered simply: "I love them all."

That seemed to stop him in his tracks. I was certain, moreover, that he was not as familiar with Giono as he pretended to be. What he wanted to tell me, undoubtedly, was that the Giono of a certain period was much better than the Giono of another. The "better" Giono would, of course, have been *his* Giono. This is the sort of small talk which keeps literary circles in a perpetual ferment.

When *Colline* appeared it was as if the whole world recognized this man Giono. This happened again when *Que ma joie demeure* came out. It probably happened a number of times. At any rate, whenever this happens, whenever a book wins immediate universal acclaim, it is somehow taken for granted that the book is a true reflection of the author. It is as though until that moment the man did not exist. Or perhaps it is admitted that the man existed but the writer did not. Yet the writer exists even before the man, paradoxically. The man would never have become what he did unless there was in him the creative germ. He lives the life which he will record in words. He dreams his life before he lives it; he dreams it *in order to live it.*

In their first "successful" work some authors give such a full image of themselves that no matter what they say later this image endures, dominates, and often obliterates all succeeding ones. The same thing happens sometimes in our first encounter with another individual. So strongly does the personality of the other register itself in such moments that ever afterwards, no matter how much the person alters, or reveals his other aspects, this first image is the one which endures. Sometimes it is a blessing that one is able to retain this original full image; other times it is a rank injustice inflicted upon the one we love.

That Giono is a man of many facets I would not think of denying. That, like all of us, he has his good side and his bad side, I would not deny either. In Giono's case it happens that with every book he produces he reveals himself fully. The revelation is given in every sentence. He is always himself and he is always giving of himself. This is one of the rare qualities he possesses, one which distinguishes him from a host of lesser writers. Moreover, like Picasso, I can well imagine him saying: "Is it necessary that everything I do prove a masterpiece?" Of him, as of Picasso, I would say that the "masterpiece" was the creative act itself and not a particular work which happened to please a large audience and be accepted as the very body of Christ.

Supposing you have an image of a man and then one day, quite by accident, you come upon him in a strange mood, find him behaving or speaking in a way you have never believed him capable of. Do you reject this unacceptable aspect of the man or do you incorporate it in a larger picture of him? Once he revealed himself to you completely, you thought. Now you find him quite other. Are *you* at fault or is *he?*

I can well imagine a man for whom writing is a life's task revealing so many aspects of himself, as he goes along, that he baffles and bewilders his readers. And the more baffled and bewildered they are by the protean character of his being, the less qualified are they, in my opinion, to talk of "masterpieces" or of "revelation." A mind open and receptive would at least wait until the last word had been written. That at least. But it is the nature of little minds to kill a man off before his time, to arrest his development at that point which is most comfortable for one's peace of mind. Should an author set himself a problem which is not to the liking or the understanding of your little man, what happens? Why, the classic avowal: "He's not the writer he used to be!" Meaning, always, "he's not the writer *I know*."

As creative writers go, Giono is still a comparatively young man. There will be more ups and downs, from the standpoint of carping critics. He will be dated and re-dated, pigeonholed and re-pigeonholed, resurrected and re-resurrected—until the final dead line. And those who enjoy this game, who identify it with the art of interpretation, will of course undergo many changes themselves—in themselves. The diehards will make sport of him until the very end. The tender idealists will be disillusioned time and again, and will also find their beloved again and again. The skeptics will always be on the fence, if not the old one another one, but on the fence.

Whatever is written about a man like Giono tells you more about the critic or interpreter than about Giono. For, like the song of the world, Giono goes on and on and on. The critic perpetually pivots around his rooted, granulated self. Like the girouette, he tells which way the wind is blowing—but he is not of the wind nor of the airs. He is like an automobile without spark plugs.

A simple man who does not boast of his opinions but who is

capable of being moved, a simple man who is devoted, loving and loyal is far better able to tell you about a writer like Giono than the learned critics. Trust the man whose heart is moved, the man whose withers can still be wrung. Such men are with the writer when he orders his creation. They do not desert the writer when he moves in ways beyond their understanding. Becoming is their silence and instructive. Like the very wise, they know how to hold themselves in abeyance.

"Each day," says Miguel de Unamuno, "I believe less and less in the social question, and in the political question, and in the moral question, and in all the other questions that people have invented in order that they shall not have to face resolutely the only real question that exists—the *human* question. So long as we are not facing this question, all that we are now doing is simply making a noise so that we shall not hear it."

Giono is one of the writers of our time who faces this human question squarely. It accounts for much of the disrepute in which he has found himself. Those who are active on the periphery regard him as a renegade. In their view he is not playing the game. Some refuse to take him seriously because he is "only a poet." Some admit that he has a marvellous gift for narrative but no sense of reality. Some believe that he is writing a legend of his region and not the story of our time. Some wish us to believe that he is only a dreamer. He is all these things and more. He is a man who never detaches himself from the world, even when he is dreaming. Particularly the world of human beings. In his books he speaks as father, mother, brother, sister, son and daughter. He does not depict the human family against the background of nature, he makes the human family a part of nature. If there is suffering and punishment, it is because of the operation of divine law through nature. The cosmos which Giono's figures inhabit is strictly ordered. There is room in it for all the irrational elements. It does not give, break or weaken because the fictive characters who compose it sometimes move in contradiction of or defiance to the laws which govern our everyday world. Giono's world possesses a reality far more understandable, far more durable than the one we accept as world reality. Tolstoy expressed the nature of this other deeper reality in his last work:

This then is everything that I would like to say: I would say to you that we are living in an age and under conditions that cannot last and that, come what may, we are obliged to choose a new path. And in order to follow it, it is not necessary for us to invent a new religion nor to discover new scientific theories in order to explain the meaning of life or art as a guide. Above all it is useless to turn back again to some special activity; it is necessary to adopt one course alone to free ourselves from the superstitions of false Christianity and of state rule.

Let each one realize that he has no right, nor even the possibility, to organize the life of others; that he should lead his own life according to the supreme religious law revealed to him, and as soon as he has done this, the present order will disappear; the order that now reigns among the so-called Christian nations, the order that has caused the whole world to suffer, that conforms so little to the voice of conscience and that renders humanity more miserable every day. Whatever you are: ruler, judge, landlord, worker, or tramp, reflect and have pity on your soul. No matter how clouded your brain has become through power, authority and riches, no matter how maltreated and harassed you are by poverty and humiliation, remember that you possess and manifest, as we all do, a divine spirit which now asks clearly: Why do you martyrize yourself and cause suffering to everyone with whom you come in contact? Understand, rather, who you really are, how truly insignificant and vulnerable is the being you call you, and which you recognize in your own shape, and to what extent, on the contrary, the real you is immeasurably your spiritual self—and having understood this, begin to live each moment to accomplish your true mission in life revealed to you by a universal wisdom, the teachings of Christ, and your own conscience. Put the best of yourself into increasing the emancipation of your spirit from the illusions of the flesh and into love of your neighbor, which is one and the same thing. As soon as you begin to live this way you will experience the joyous feeling of liberty and well-being. You will be surprised to find that the same exterior objectives which preoccupied you and which were far from realization, will no longer stand in the way of your greatest possible happiness. And if you are unhappy—I know you are unhappy—ponder upon what I have stated here. It is not merely imagined by me but is the result of the reflections and beliefs of the most enlightened human hearts and spirits; therefore, realize that this is the one and only way to free yourself from your unhappiness and to discover the greatest possible good that life can offer. This then is what I would like to say to my brothers, before I die.[5]

31

Notice that Tolstoy speaks of "the greatest possible happiness" and "the greatest possible good." I feel certain that these are the two goals which Giono would have humanity attain. Happiness! Who, since Maeterlinck has dwelt at any length on this state of being? Who talks nowadays of "the greatest good"? To talk of happiness and of the good is now suspect. They have no place in our scheme of reality. Yes, there is endless talk of the political question, the social question, the moral question. There is much agitation, but nothing of moment is being accomplished. Nothing *will* be accomplished until the human being is regarded as a whole, until he is first looked upon as a human being and not a political, social or moral animal.

As I pick up Giono's last book—*Les Ames Fortes*—to scan once again the complete list of his published works, I am reminded of the visit I made to his home during his absence. Entering the house I was instantly aware of the profusion of books and records. The place seemed to be overflowing with spiritual provender. In a bookcase, high up near the ceiling, were the books he had written. Even then, eleven years ago, an astounding number for a man of his age. I look again, now, at the list as it is given opposite the title page of his last work, published by Gallimard. How many I have still to read! And how eloquent are the titles alone! *Solitude de la Pitié*, *Le Poids du Ciel*, *Naissance de l'Odyssée*, *Le Serpent d'Etoiles*, *Les Vraies Richesses*, *Fragments d'un Déluge*, *Fragments d'un Paradis*, *Présentation de Pan*... A secret understanding links me to these unknown works. Often, at night, when I go into the garden for a quiet smoke, when I look up at Orion and the other constellations, all so intimate a part of Giono's world, I wonder about the contents of these books I have not read, which I promise myself I will read in moments of utter peace and serenity, for to "crowd them in" would be an injustice to Giono. I imagine him also walking about in his garden, stealing a look at the stars, meditating on the work in hand, bracing himself for renewed conflicts with editors, critics and public. In such moments it does not seem to me that he is far away, in a country called France. He is in Manosque, and between Manosque and Big Sur there is an affinity which abolishes time and space. He is in that garden where the spirit of his mother still reigns, not far from the manger in which he was born and where his father who taught him so much worked at the bench as a cobbler. His garden has a wall around it; here there is none. That is one of the differences between the Old World and the New. But there is no wall between Giono's spirit and my own. That is what draws me to him—the openness of his spirit. One feels it the moment one opens his books. One tumbles in drugged, intoxicated, rapt.

Giono gives us the world he lives in, a world of dream, passion and reality. It is French, yes but that would hardly suffice to describe it. It is of a certain region of France, yes, but that does not define it. It is distinctly Jean Giono's world and none other. If you are are a kindred spirit you recognize it immediately, no matter where you were born or raised, what language you speak, what customs you have adopted, what tradition you follow. A man does not have to be Chinese, nor even a poet, to recognize immediately such spirits as Lao Tsu and Li Po. In Giono's work what every sensitive, full-blooded individual ought to be able to recognize at once is "the song of the world." For me this song, of which each new book gives endless refrains and variations, is far more precious, far more stirring, far more poetic, than the "Song of Songs." It is intimate, personal, cosmic, untrammeled—and ceaseless. It contains the notes of the lark, the nightingale, the thrush; it contains the whir of the planets and the almost inaudible wheeling of the constellations; it contains the sobs, cries, shrieks and wails of wounded mortal souls as well as the laughter and ululations of the blessed; it contains the seraphic music of the angelic hosts and the howls of the damned. In addition to this pandemic music Giono gives the whole gamut of color, taste, smell and feel. The most inanimate objects yield their mysterious vibrations. The philosophy behind this symphonic production has no name: its function is to liberate, to keep open all the sluices of the soul, to encourage speculation, adventure and passionate worship.

"Be what thou art, only be it to the utmost!" That is what it whispers.

Is this French?

NOTES

1. *Politics of the Unpolitical*, by Herbert Read, Routledge, London, 1946.
2. From *Democratic Vistas*.
3. *The Reading of Books*, Scribner's, New York, 1947.
4. *Et bien mieux qu' Ossendoivski!*
5. *The Law of Love and the Law of Violence*.

The Solitude of Compassion

They were sitting against the gate at the station. Looking at the
rattletrap coach and the rain-slick road, they did not know which
way to go. The winter afternoon was right there in the white, flat
mud like a piece of linen fallen from a drying rack.

The larger of the two got up. He searched on both sides of his
big velour hussard pants; then he picked with the end of his fingers
at the little carpenter's pocket. The carriage driver climbed into the
seat. He clicked his tongue and the horses perked up their ears. The
man cried: "Wait." Then he said to his companion: "Come," and the
other came. He floated, all thin in a threadbare shepherd's greatcoat.
His neck stuck out of the sackcloth, emaciated like a piece of iron.

"Where's it going?" asked the larger man.

"To town."

"How much is it?"

"Ten cents."

"Get in," said the large man.

He bent down, spread the folds of the greatcoat, lifted the leg of
the other man up onto the step:

"Get in," he told him; "Just try, old man."

35

+ + +

It took time for the young lady to gather up her boxes and move herself. She had a fine, white, wide-lined nose and she knew that her nose was visible under the rice powder, so she looked a little to the side with almost an angry expression, and it was for this reason that the large man said to her: "Excuse me, Mademoiselle." Across from him there was a chubby, delicate lady in a coat with fur on the collar and the sleeves; a travelling salesman who pressed himself against the lady, and who, to better touch her with his elbow on her lower breast, put his thumb in the armhole of his vest.

"Just lean there," said the large man while raising his shoulder.

The other lowered his head and set it on his shoulder.

He had beautiful blue eyes that were as immobile as stagnant water.

They went slowly because it was uphill. The blue of his eyes followed the passage of the trees, unceasingly, as if to count them. Then they crossed flat fields, and there was no longer anything in the window except the monotonous grey sky. His regard grew as fixed as a nail. He was going to tumble right onto the chubby woman; but he seemed to be looking through her, farther on, very sadly, it was like a sheep's gaze.

The lady pulled her fur collar together. The salesman touched the front of his pants to see if they were well buttoned. The lady tugged at her skirt as if to lengthen it.

This gaze was always fixed on the same spot. He was going to pieces, he was causing pus to form like a thorn.

The lady wiped her lips with the skin of her glove; she dried her lips which shone with soft saliva. The travelling salesman touched the front of his pants again; then he unfolded his arm again like someone who has a cramp. He tried to make contact with the gaze resembling stagnant water; but he lowered his eyes, then he put his hand seemingly over his heart. His wallet was still there. At least he felt its shape and its thickness.

A shadow filled the carriage; the little town greeted the avenue to the station with two arms of houses that were covered with spots. On one side it presented the "Hotel of Commerce and Gardens" and on the other side three bitterly competing bakeries.

+ + +

Monsieur le Curé* cleaned his pipe in the offertory basin; the ashtray was down below on the edge of the prie-dieu. He put the warm pipe in the box. Now he had to classify by roads and houses those volumes of the Religious Evenings which he was going to distribute to subscribers. He was missing three copies. He lifted up the books and an edition of The Cross that lay open. Eventually he found them there under the packet of pig tripe which his brother had just brought. "It is no longer necessary…" A cover was spotted. He tilted it to see if the spots were visible, if by slanting it…or, very well, he only had to give it to Madame Puret the lamplady: she can hardly see; she always has her fingers covered with oil; she will think that she did it.

There was also, there, on the floor, left by Adolphe, a spot of stable manure with the print of a heel in it. Monsieur le Curé stood up and with little flicks of the point of his shoe pushed the filth over to the hearth.

"Martha, someone rang."

---

* Curé = parish priest

"What?" asked Martha opening the kitchen door.

"I said someone rang."

The thin lace of the apron on the servant covered her large breasts and belly.

"Again. You, too, Monsieur, you can go see who it is. Always going up, always going down, me, with my legs...my emphysema... You will see in the end, in the end."

Someone rang again.

"Go and see for yourself. If it is nothing much you can take care of it down there. In this weather the people who come up to see me get everything dirty."

She had a face that was all moist with fat.

"I was setting sheets of fat," she said. "The pantry is too high. One slipped and I caught it on my cheek."

✛ ✛ ✛

"Here I am," called the Curé from the hallway. Then he turned the locks and opened the door.

"Hello Monsieur," said the large man.

The thin man with the blue eyes stood in back shivering in his greatcoat.

"We don't give handouts," said the Curé looking at them.

The large man took off his hat. The thin man raised a hand into the air while staring at the Curé.

"Do you have some little job?" said the large man.

"A job?"

And the Curé looked like he was reflecting, but at the same time he gently pushed the door.

"A job."

He opened the door completely.

"Enter," he said.

The large man who had put on his hat removed it again quickly.

"Thank you very much, Monsieur le Curé, thank you very much."

And he scraped his shoes on the scraper, and he entered bending his back a little, despite the high frame of the door.

The other did not say anything, he came in standing straight in his dirty shoes; he followed the Curé's gestures with the cold sadness of his blue eyes.

+ + +

They entered the spacious hallway, because at one time the parish had been the home of some landowners. Then came a tiled courtyard, and to this courtyard stairways were attached which ascended in great tiled swoops.

"Wait for me here," the Curé remembered while looking at their muddy shoes.

He went up.

The large man silently produced a little smile.

"You see, it is going to work," he said. "The twenty cents that we spent…"

+ + +

"Martha…" said the Curé, then immediately:

"What are you doing there?"

It was a hot plate set on the table of white wood and in it the tripe sizzled with bits of purple liver like flowers and rice on the stalk.

"It's a picoche," said Martha.

And she began to pour a thin stream of thick wine with the smell of wood root. The bubbling grease was silenced.

"Is that for tonight?" asked the Curé.

"Yes."

"Tell me, Martha, can you guess what I have come up with? What if we used them to fix the end of the pump?"

"He would have to go down into the well," said Martha as she measured the line of wine.

"But of course," said the Curé.

She did not say a thing, then she raised the neck with a clean sweep; she carried the plate over to the fire.

"And you will find someone. Someone who will go down? You know what the plumber said. He did not want to kill himself. It is an old well, and so, in this weather, you will really find someone?"

"Listen: there are two men down below asking for something to do. They look like men in need."

"Well we should make the most of them," said Martha, "because you know that the plumber will never go down. He told me so. If they are in need, then we should make the most of them."

"This is what's the matter," said the Curé. "We have a pump, and the iron end was stuck against the side of the well. The attachment, or the attachments must have slipped. The end is unstuck, you could say, and it sucks up thin air. It is suspended like that from the bolts on top and that could have come completely out. I have the attachments right here. You have to go down…"

"Is the well deep?" asked the large man.

"No," said the Curé, "No. Yes. At least not very, you know, it is a house well: fifteen, twenty meters at most."

"Is it far?"

"No. It is right there."

The Curé walked to the side of the courtyard and the large man followed him, and the other followed in his greatcoat. There was a gate in the wall and, below, a trough of old stone worn by water. He opened the gate, the hinges squealed and two or three scales of rust fell on the tiles.

"There you see."

The well blew a bitter breath of nocturnal plants and deep water. There was the "sssglouf" of a detached stone that fell. The Curé, very much in back, leaned and at the same time pulled back his rump, and one heard his toes slosh in his shoes.

"There you see."

He seemed as if he wanted to excuse himself.

"As there are two of you," he said.

Then the large man looked at his companion. He was there still floating in his grey greatcoat. He did not have a face except for his eyes, cold blue eyes, always fixed on the black soutane of the Curé but looking through it and beyond it like the sad soul of the world.

He trembled and painfully swallowed his saliva with great bobbings of his Adam's apple.

"Good, Monsieur le Curé," said the large man, "that will do, I work alone, but that will do."

Martha appeared on the balcony of the gallery.

"Monsieur le Curé, it is about time for your music lesson."

At just this moment someone rang. He went and opened the door: it was a little blond youth in a beautiful wool coat.

"Go on up, Monsieur René," said the Curé. "I am coming."

He came back toward the men.

"The wall might be just a little bit bad," he said.

+ + +

"Set yourself there, old man," said the large man.

There was a door in the back of the courtyard. Behind it they could hear rabbits running and crying out.

"Set yourself there. Sit down. You are not cold, too cold?…"

Then he sat to one side and began untying his shoes.

"I prefer to do it barefoot. You catch yourself with your toenails…"

Then he unbuttoned his hussard pants and pulled them off.

"Barelegged works better, and besides they're heavy. Put them on, and they will keep you warm."

The exhalation of the well steamed-up into the cold air of the courtyard.

"If I need to, I will call you," just when he stepped on the rim.

He still held himself up by his hands and you could see his head. He looked down into the blackness; and you could tell that he was busy trying to secure his feet.

"I see the holes old man. It's going to fly."

He disappeared.

+ + +

One heard the sound of a harmonium: a spiral of ascending notes which stuck together in threes and slowly darted, so it seemed, towards the sky like the swaying of a serpent's head.

It was played rather well by Monsieur le Curé, then taken up again after a silence by the wide hands of Monsieur René.

The daylight faded.

On the wooden gallery, up there on the second floor, there was a row of cactus plants and a pot with a tuft of violets. The man looked at the flowers. The night flowed into the courtyard like water from a fountain; soon the flowers were no longer visible; the night rose up to the third floor.

The man stood up. He approached the well, looked for the opening by feeling with his hand. He leaned over. Down below one could hear, it seemed, a sort of scraping.

"Hey," he called.

"Hey," responded the other from below.

It came after a short pause, stifled by a cushion of air.

"Take care of yourself," said the man.

"Yes," replied the voice. Then it asked, "and you up there. How goes it?"

The man went back and sat down at the moment when Martha opened the door and appeared in the gallery of the second floor with a lamp in her hand.

"You can see the way Monsieur René?... Close the door."

The blond youth closed the door. Martha looked out into the courtyard.

"I think that they have gone," she said.

✦ ✦ ✦

The large man walked in shadow. His muddy feet were heard squishing on the cold tiles.

"Are you there?" he asked.

"Yes."

"Give me my pants. It's over."

"It's cold out," he added once he was dressed again.

43

The house was all silent except for the sizzling of a fried fish which flowed from the second floor.

He called out:

"Monsieur le Curé."

The frying kept him from hearing. He cried out:

"Monsieur le Curé."

"What?" asked Martha.

"It's done," said the man.

"What?" asked Martha again.

"The pump."

"Ah! Good, I will come and see."

She went back into the kitchen and tried to give a push on the pump to the well. The water flowed. Monsieur le Curé was reading by the stove, and there was the sizzling of the frying.

"It's flowing," she said.

He hardly raised his eyes.

"Good. Go pay them."

"How much should I give them? After all it was done quickly."

"…and close the door tightly…"

But she accompanied them, watched them leave, then firmly set the latch, pushed the lock, and set the bar.

A cold and tenacious rain was falling.

Under the streetlight the man opened his hand. It was ten cents. The blue eyes looked at the little coin and the hand all marked with scrapes and mud.

"You will get tired," he said, "I am a chain around your neck, me, sick. You will get tired, leave me."

"No," said the large man. "Come."

Prelude to Pan

It happened on the fourth of September, the year of those big storms, that year when there was misfortune for everyone in our land.

If you will recall, it began with a sort of landslide by Toussière in which more than fifty pines were knocked head over heels. The ravine carried away the long cadavers of the trees, and it made a lot of noise... It was a shame to see all of those trunks of good wood thrown against the rocks, and all that getting washed out in shreds like meat from a sick person. Then there was that gushing of the spring at Frontfroit. Do you recall? The high prairie was suddenly all wet, then that spring mouth which opened up under the grasses, and you heard the black water splashing, then this retching which took hold of it on the mountain and in the valley which wailed under the heavy load of cold water.

Those two things made people talk; they were entranced by them. More than one person got up in the middle of the night and went barefoot over to the window to listen, in the depths of the darkness, to the mountain quaking like a sick child. Still we had a little peace.

But the days were not in their usual health. On the border of Léchau a green fog floated; there was this fog stuck to all the corners of the mountain as if the wind was heavy with sea grasses. Towards Planpre it smelled like crushed gentian. One day a forest girl came with a beautiful mushroom, larger than a hat, pale and spotted with black like a dead man's head.

All of that should have set us on our guard, and, to tell the truth, we were on guard against all of it; but life is life; go ahead try and stop the flow, you get used to anything, even fear.

The fourth of September is our votive festival. It made our reputation, as they say. From my younger years it united three or four communes. They came from Vaugnières, Glandages, Montbran, crossing the ridge… At the time in question they had largely stopped celebrating with us; there was no longer anyone coming but folk from the high farms, tall woodsmen, and shepherds who came on the sly and entered the village in the evening to have a glass. They left their herds alone on the Oches' pastures.

As I said to you, there was a great calm. Above us there was a round patch of blue sky all spread out, perfectly neat, all clean. On the circumference of the horizon there was a thick bar of heavy, purple clouds; it was there mornings and evenings, without moving, always the same, breaking the backs of the mountains.

"It will get the others," is what they said.

"It should rain in Trièves."

"It should be bad on la Drôme."

We said it, but even so we looked at the round blueness which weighed on the village like a millstone.

Now that we know, we know that it was the mark, the sign, that we were destined for something, that by this circle they had want-ed to indicate our village and make it shine in the sun in order to designate it for evil. So it was, we were happy.

"The weather purged itself before. You will see that it will be nice for the festival."

"It should be for once."

The son of the blacksmith went around to all the houses with a list, and one gave, perhaps a hundred cents, perhaps three francs, so that our festival would be a nice festival and not make us be ashamed. By the school there was already a booth which smelled of caramel candy.

For a night or two there were noises in the sky.

"That is, if, all the same..."

But no, the mornings were blond with ripe grass; the wind smelled of gramineal, there was the circle of blue filled with sun-shine which fooled us. The ground was warm beneath our feet and elastic like a fruit.

This fourth of September then, one opened the shutters, and it was fine weather. The people from the Café du Peuple had planted a May tree before their door, a young pine that was all glistening. In its branches were hung the red scarf which one won at boule, the blue scarf which was the prize for the girls' race, and the money which was the prize for the men's race. All of them were floating on a stream of joyful, scented air that played like a young kid.

The folk from the Café du Centre had installed trestles all the way down to the Liberty tree. The washhouse was filled with bot-tles that were cooling in the water. The baker had ordered a case of tarts from his cousin du Champsaur, and he was on his doorstep waiting for them saying to people passing by:

"You know, I am going to have tarts."

And we thought:

"Good, that will be a good dessert."

Apollonia waited for her nephews du Trièves. Brother Antoine was supposed to come from Coriardes with his whole family. The boule players from Trabuech wrote down their names and they were the great players... From Montama six came, from Montbran three, and we knew that the shepherds from Oches would come, but we did not say anything.

The first rough characters that were seen were the Coriardes folk. They put the mule in the stable, looking under it without a word, and, immediately afterwards, the father whispered to Antoine:

"You have to arrange for us to sleep here tonight, we do not want to go back at night."

Then the father said:

"We'll have something strong to drink."

The Coriardes folk were asked what they had.

"Nothing."

And there was a black mystery in their eyes which stayed for more than two hours.

The folk from Trièves were soaking.

"It is raining on the ridge, quite a lot..."

Only at that moment we were not thinking on our feet any longer. There was in the sky, like a hand spreading the pile of clouds, a little breeze flowing which smelled like meadow sweet. The sun spread out on the earth and began resting while blotting out the clouds. There only remained a threat in the direction of Montama where the clouds were still shining and dark like a heap of eggplants.

The Café du Centre was filled to the rafters. In the kitchen there was the sound of dishes and water so that you would think a stream was flowing through there. People were inundated with beer and wine. On the floor, when you moved your feet, they made a mark in the coating of spilled beer and wine. Outside there were people all the way to the Liberty tree. Marie went to the washhouse and filled her arms with streaming bottles of fresh water, and she carried them, shivering, because they wet her breast and in time the water ran down onto her stomach.

When she arrived to serve them, people pinched her haunches and slapped her rump, and there were even those who stuck an arm all the way up her dress.

"Ah, leave it there, it's so warm," she said.

For drink, there were already those who were sick and who sang "Poor Peasant." Others quickly left the benches to go throw up in a corner. There were those who laughed about who knows what, but with such laughs! Those who pissed sitting up, and who became serious again when they felt themselves moistened between the legs. Then they began laughing and drinking again. In the Café du Peuple it was the same, except for in a corner in the back at the little table where the trio from Trièves were. They had crossed the ridge in the morning. It was not hard in September, but they said: "It's funny. It's not natural. Who knows?..."

They had pipes and big glasses, and they tried to dispel their uneasiness.

At noon something happened which would pull everyone out of there. They were in the middle of discussing the defeat of Polyte at boule, and my Polyte was all somber, right in the middle, chewing his mustache. We spoke as if we were haranguing the housewives...

For the youths, again it was easy. They were excited with their hands on the servants' buttocks, nothing to do but to sniff the scent of their wives. It made them rise, but the others would have to be told about it!

"Go on big bags!" "Then come!" "You are already well taken care of." And "at your age" and "You are cute, go" and even men slapping women and women slapping men, sort of among family.

And those who responded:

"Go to bed, you old bloodsucker."

But, even so there were those who got up and left.

Finally, there was room once again with empty spaces in the road and in the two cafés where people were dining. There was also in the sky, like a bird, a thick silence, heavy and solitary. In this silence there was not a puff of air nor the sound of a footstep, not a whisper of grass, nor the hum of a wasp; there was only silence, round and weighty, filled with sun like a ball of fire.

It was in the middle of this silence that a man arrived by the forest path. He came in the shadow of the houses. He seemed to enfold himself in their shadow. He took two steps, then looked around, then he took several more light steps along the walls. He saw our poplar tree. Then he dared to cross a great swathe of sun, and he came towards the tree. He stayed there for a moment sniffing. He checked the wind. He had a round back, like a hunted beast. With his hand he caressed the old skin of our tree. In an instant he lowered a branch and placed his head in the leaves to smell them. Finally, he moved on to the Café du Peuple. He drew back the curtain and softly entered.

I saw it all from my window. I was just about to take my siesta. The party did not mean much to me, I was alone in the house, as you know.

Now, the story is Antoine's, who served him.

He was thin and all dried out, seemingly ageless. He was without a vest in his shirt of blue thread like the sky; he had rolled up his sleeves and his wrinkled, black elbows were visible like the wounds of branches on a tree trunk. He had hair on his chest like a sheep dog.

He asked for water. Nothing more. And he said:

"I will pay for it."

Once it had been said it did not seem like something that one could contradict. He was given his water. He wanted it in a bucket.

Antoine told me about it:

"I went into the kitchen, and I was very curious. I did not say anything to the folk from Trièves who were eating there; I did not say anything to the woman, but I looked at him through a tear in the curtain. He even drank from the wooden bucket like an animal. Then he took three pine cones out of his pocket, took them apart on the table, and began eating the nuts. He picked them up with his fingertips, and chewed them with the ends of his teeth. From where I was watching him, he seemed like a big squirrel."

The noon meal lasted for hours because they had prepared all the foods in creation. First they had taken sausages out of the vat of oil and laid them there on the plate, white and fat, like big caterpillars. They had put on a rooster to braze, and the rabbits stewed in their own blood. They had killed goats. Everywhere it smelled like crushed meat and dead grasses. They had drunk various wines...wine from the mountainside, wine from the rocky area, a two-year-old wine...

"This one, what do you say?"

"Ah, my friend!..."

Old wine from fine bottles, one only had to reach out one's hand, even without a candle, and it was there right away. The serving folk brought the bottles down. That was the festival in our town. They crammed their mouths with pieces of white chicken meat which hung from the end of their forks like strips of ash bark.

In the end, in the houses, one could smell all of the smells, except for the good ones.

It could have been about three-thirty when the man, having finished his meal, got up. He paid.

Antoine did not want any money for the water. The man said: "For the corner of your establishment where I sat."

And he forced him to take a coin. But as he was going out, the entire hoard of Boniface's men arrived, blocked the door, and came in knocking things over with:

"Hello, everyone!"

And there was the smell of sausage.

This hoard was made up of the absolutely biggest woodsmen.

The man faintly tried to pass between them; then he fell back into his shadowy corner, and, with all of the other big men stationed in the middle, he no longer dared.

He was like, so it seemed, a beast caught in a trap; he turned his head in all directions to see which way to go. His beautiful, distraught eyes were supplicating.

Besides, all that is according to Antoine and perhaps his memory is foggy about what happened next.

Thus, the man was back in his corner where there were shadows, and the café began filling up again.

With regard to myself, it was almost at this very moment that I got up from my siesta, and I recalled that my first task was to go to the skylight in the attic to check the sky. The blue had grown smaller. And more of the clouds were piled up over Montama, which still remained immobile and damned hard. There were two or three bad clouds which extended over the mountain to see what we were doing.

"It will not come over this evening," I said.

And in fact...

As for me, I had gotten up right away at four o'clock. There was only one thing to do: go to Antoine's, or to the "Center," which, it is understood, meant the same thing.

That is how I arrived when it had already begun.

Upon approaching I said to myself:

"They are arguing."

I heard Boniface bawling.

I entered:

They were all turned towards the back of the room, towards something which the shadow revealed after a moment, the man. He emerged from the shadow as if from water. I do not know if it was an effect of the day which turned around the village and came up a bit abruptly, or if this man's strength radiated outwards and off-set the shadow. But, the fact is that I saw him all of a sudden. He was standing very sadly, overwhelmed by a great thought which shaded his eyes to black. On his shoulder a wood dove had set itself. And it was with those two, him and the dove, that Boniface, lost in his wine, was angry.

It seemed that it had begun humorously enough. At first, I have to say: the entire troop of big men, woodsmen of size XL, up there beside Garnezier, arrived straight out of the high woods after more than a hundred days of solitary encampment. They came in after having lived for a hundred days, I tell you, with just the sky and the rocks for companions. The forest was not their companion: they were killing it. Which they had to do, even so, just to live! This friendship which they were forced to have with the great, steely sky, with the hard air, with this cold ground like dead flesh, gave them the desire to kiss the trees like friends, but then, look, they were there to kill them. I am explaining it poorly, what do you want?… It was a little, if you don't mind my saying so, as if you who love Bertha, I know it, and she merits it, they required you to kill her so that you could live, and to make puddings with her blood. Excuse me, it was a manner of speaking, but now you know.

Well, to get back to those men, the things contained in their desire and in their love was transformed into cruelty towards men and animals. They were there with their beards like moss, with their gestures accustomed to the open air, and that were larger than ours. Boniface had brought the little wood dove in the pocket of his velour vest. He had gotten it into his head, up there, to tame it, and because each time that he released it, it spurted around the cabin, knocking over the candle, and flew like a crazy woman against the window curtain; it had broken one of its shoulders.

Yes.

Can you see it?

That was pretty bad, and he did it coldly, deliberately, of his free will, with his big hands which are like burdock leaves. Yes, he pressed the grey bird into his palm, and he twisted its wing until he heard the bone crack. What do you expect?

So it was there, the poor beast, all crippled, dragging its wing as a dead weight; it was there with this dead thing that weighed on it. Just like that, in one gesture he had taken away from it all of the sky, all of the goodness of flying through the air at the speed of the wind… It was there, dragging itself across the table in the spewed out wine.

There he was, propped up on his chair with his full stomach overflowing his pants, laughing. He laughed, and he looked at the poor little thing. He had weighed his strength against it; and of a clump of feathers, he had made this awkward little ball which stumbled against the glasses, which was there dragging about and crying out. When it drew itself away from him, he hit it with the back of his hand, and sent it back amid the spilled wine. And then the bird tried to open its wings, and the wound on its shoulder cracked, it let out a long cry of complaint, and it remained for a long time with its beak open, all trembling with its head crazed.

When this had happened three times, the man in the back said: "Let that creature be."

From the surprise of hearing a voice in a corner where he had thought that no one or nothing else was, Boniface turned around. And the dove was touched by that voice too. And that voice must have been a little hope for it. It must have known the voice from instinct, because seemingly right away, there it was gathering itself together. There it was suppressing its pain with a stroke of will. There it was stretching suddenly the expanse of its feathers and with a cooing threw itself towards the voice. It was all dirty with wine. One heard it, there, beside the man, cooing for joy, and one also heard the man. He was speaking to the dove. He spoke to it in the language of doves and the dove responded to him with its sad voice.

"Who is that?" Boniface asked.

Now the café was filled with people, but no one knew who it was —that man.

It was at that very moment that I came in. It was at that very moment also that one of those clouds, earlier all white, all massive like a cake, passed over the village, reflecting the sun. A ray of light struck the panes of glass. The back of the café was lit up. The man was visible.

"Leave us alone. You, boy, give me back my bird," said Boniface extending a hand.

The man had the dove on his shoulder. He turned towards it and spoke to it in the language of doves. He sighed. Boniface's large hand was still outstretched beside him.

"Come on…"

"I am keeping it," said the man.

"So!…" Boniface just had the chance to say he was so overwhelmed by the calmness of the man. "So that's it!" and he stood up making the chair creak. He was in our drinking room standing like the trunk of an oak tree.

And he stood there, because the other went on in his little, calm voice. Once you had heard that voice you could not move either your arms or your legs. You asked yourself: "But haven't I already heard that somewhere before?" And you had your head filled with trees and birds, rain and wind, and the trembling of the earth.

"I am keeping it," said the man. "It belongs to me. By what right did you go and take it, and twist it? By what right did you, strong, solid, ruin this gray creature? Tell me! It has blood, it does, like you do; it has blood of the same color, and it has a right to the sun and the wind like you do. You have no more right than this creature. The same things were given to you and to it. You take enough with your nose, you take enough with your eyes. You must have ruined things to be as fat as that…in the middle of life. You have not understood that up until now it has been a miracle that you could go on killing and murdering, and then live just the same, your mouth filled with blood? You have not understood that it has been a miracle that you could digest all of the blood and all of the pain that you've drunk in. But still, why?

We were like dead logs lined up along the roadside.

"That man is crazy," said Boniface.

"No, he is not crazy," said the man. "It is you who are crazy. Isn't it insane to murder that, look!"

He gently took the dove down from his shoulder. He had soft gestures with it. It was there, in his hands cooing happily. And he displayed the poor dead wing, and he made everyone see, hanging, lifeless, like something withdrawn from the world. And then we said: "Oh! Oh!" all together. And it was not to Boniface's glory.

"One more time," the big man said to him, "are you going to give my bird back to me?"

"I told you, no. I am keeping it. You treat it badly."

Then we looked at them because, Boniface, we knew him. He was not too bad a chap, but when one opposed him, when one went too much against him, my faith, he was not the last one to take out his fists. And we thought:

"This stranger has gone a little too far."

Antoine appeared in the kitchen doorway.

The drinking room is not very big; with a step Boniface could be at the back of it. He took this step, he raised his arm which was like a big branch, his fist at the end like a gourd…

And he remained like that with his fist in the air.

The man had set the dove back on his shoulder. He made a little murmur towards it, as if to tell it not to fear, to stay there. And he turned his goat's face towards us with his two big, sad, illuminated eyes. He stood reflecting a moment with an eye on us. Then he decided.

"I would say that you need to be taught a bit of a lesson," he said. "Maybe in the mix you will find clarity of heart."

He pointed his index finger slowly at Antoine and said to him: "Go fetch your accordion."

Like that.

And there was, all around, a great silence from everyone; except for outside where the festival continued to moo like a big cow. And for myself, who was there, I can tell you, it was exactly as if I had a mouthful of cement that was drying, and for the others it must have been the same, and for Boniface too. No one made a gesture, not even with their lips. The weight of the entire earth was upon us.

Up above the café we heard Antoine's step as he went to fetch his accordion from his room, then it was on the stairs, and then he reappeared.

He was there with the instrument between his hands. He was ready. He was awaiting the command.

"Play," said the man.

Then he began playing. Then those who were near the door saw the clouds come over.

Big Boniface let his arm fall slowly. And at this very moment he lifted a leg, gently, in the cadence and in harmony with the music which was softer than a May wind. Even so, what Antoine was busy playing was still the standard fare: the "Mie dolce amore" and his medley of songs that he had made up; but they had taken on a certain something…

Then Boniface raised his other leg, and he rounded his arms, and stuck out his haunches, then he shook his shoulders, then his beard began to flap in the movement. He was dancing.

He danced there, right in front of the man who did not take his eyes off him. He danced like he fought, against his will, with movements that were still sticky. It was like the birth-of-all dance. Then, little by little, his entire apparatus of bones and muscles, oiled with music, caught fire, and he began leaping crazily and emitting deep "han hans." His feet struck the wooden floor, his feet raised up a dust which smoked up to the level of his knees.

We were there, overwhelmed, watching. For myself, I was no longer the master of either my arms or my legs, nor of any part of my body except for my head. It was free, it could leisurely watch the shadow of the storm rise, listen to the evil wind blowing. For the others, I think, it was the same thing. I remember. We had all been wrapped up together in the same power. The most terrible thing, was this completely free head which took everything in.

In a stroke, from the moment when the man had become the leader, we all had our eyes directed upon him, and we could no longer detach them. He had a thin beard growing wild, like dry grass, long, and all tangled. Below we saw that he hardly had any chin. He had a long nose, straight and wide, and a little flat on top. It ran from the middle of his forehead down to his mouth. His beautiful lips were plump like a peeled fruit. He had beautiful oval eyes, filled with color down to the base of his eyelashes, without a spot of white, but oily like the eyes of dreaming goats. From them flowed glances that were like streams of compassion and suffering.

Now Boniface leaped like a tree that had fallen victim to the wind. And everyone was overcome with the desire to be with him, haunch to haunch. We just awaited the order.

It came in one of those regards which passed through us like a ray of light, and each took its own shape. It fell, first on André Bellin, from the hoard; and once touched, there he was up and off dancing. Then on Jacques Regotaz, then on Jean Moulin, then on Polyte des Coriardes who from the start had been repeating in a low voice: "Look. Look. Look..."

...without our knowing why. Then on the two from Trièves, then on one of the Oches, then on the serving girl Amélie. Then, at this very moment, a clap of thunder rang out like an overwhelming blow, and his gaze fell on me, I was struck as if by a rifle shot, and sent into a full dance without knowing why. And then the others, and then the others...

Things turned. Things revolved.

We had dust all the way up to our waists, and sweat flowed off us like rain, and there was a thunder of feet on the floor, and we heard the "han hans" of big Boniface, and the tables which broke, and the glass of the glasses and the bottles that we crushed under big feet with the sound that pigs make when eating chick peas, and there was a thick smell of absinthe and syrup which clasped our heads like pincers.

To tell the truth, in all of that, Antoine did not amount to much. In the middle of all the commotion we no longer heard his music. It was lost in all of that. Only we saw him by chance turning about clutching his instrument with the same fervor that the rest of us put into our dancing. It was not the music which captivated us so, but a terrible thing which had entered into our hearts along with the man's sad glances. It was stronger than us. We seemed to remember ancient gestures, old gestures from the end of man's chain of development, which the first men had made.

It had opened in our hearts like a cellar door and it had brought out all of the black forces of creation. And then, as we were now too small for it, it agitated our sack of skin like cats shut up in a linen sack. That is told in my fashion, but, I do not know how else to say it; and then, it is already quite beautiful to be able to put it like that, drawn from the mixture of all that wildness.

The dove was set on the man's shoulder. It caressed its wounded wing with its beak.

We had not danced like that since, who knows? We did not know.

And all of a sudden I felt welling up like a furor within me the abomination of all abominations.

The man advanced towards us. We made way for him. He went to the door, he spread the curtain, and he went out. Then, like a cow pulled by the forehead, Antoine straightened up and followed him. And we felt the desire to follow along too, and one after another the dance hurtled us outside, into the village like seeds. The day was the color of sulfur. It was cooking up a big storm under its cover. The clock sounded six o'clock in the evening.

The man was seated on the side of our fountain. With his hand he dipped water out of the basin and let the dove drink.

But the festival!

From the schools to the Liberty tree, the roads were filled with men drunk with our drunkenness. It revolved, it flowed, it struck the walls like a wash of water. It was like a water of men, of women and children mixed together, and it danced until it was out of strength. We had there, in the middle of our waists and the middle of our shoulders a sort of hand which pushed us and forced us on. From time to time, a door opened, and a house released its housekeeper into the dance with her soup spoon in hand or her stick of wood to add to the fire; or even the girl who was torn away from fiddling with her make-up, in a dress on the bottom and a shirt on top, and who danced right away in the middle of us, raising her arms, revealing the great tufts of red hair in her armpits. Thérèse and the Balarue son came like that, married since the night before and not having gotten up since. Yes, these two arrived naked and already sweating with their skin lustrous from their caresses. And that entered into the dough that the man kneaded with just the power of his eyes, and it entered into the dough of the great bread of evil that he was in the middle of kneading.

Now the entire village was in a trance. There were no more tables, no more trestles, no more bottles. The awning over the candy stand, torn from its posts, floated for a minute above our heads with its garnished cloth like a ship's sail; then it fell at our feet. We danced at times in a dough of caramel candy, and then it was hard to lift our feet. We danced in wine, in beer, in the piss which people let go, straight ahead without thinking in their pants or in their skirts. At times I passed by Boniface and I heard his "han han" like before. I was next to Polyte who kept repeating "Look. Look;" and other times I was with girls who had lustrous hips, and I had their moanings whispered in my ears like lost grasses.

A large bolt of lightning flew over our heads like a bird.

Then the door to the stables broke open. Mules and horses fell upon us, and colts and single-minded donkeys which were all in heat.

Then the hen houses opened up like nuts, and we received in our faces chickens and cocks that scratched with their nails into our cheeks, pigeons fell upon us like snow, the air was boiling over with all of this fowl. From the depths of the valley all of the swallows that had amassed during the preceding days before taking off, from the depths of the valley, all the swallows surged up from the willows and copses, and the warm fields. In the sky it was like a great river of the sky. It turned for a moment then dumped itself upon us, and it was a rain of swallows, and swallows were streaming, we were covered by them, we were weighed down by them, we were inundated, and wiped out as if by gushing water.

Then, all the greenery of the mountain also began boiling up like a soup. All that the forest had to offer of beasts began to sweat between the trees and the grasses. They came down the slopes like a landslide, like a mudslide. They were together, chest to chest, back to back, hair against hair, hair against shell. There were rams, foxes, wild boars, an old wolf, squirrels, forest rats, snakes which seemed like living branches, fistfuls of vipers and adders. There were eagles and hazel hens, partridges and veteran thrushes. There was a hare, I recall, who leaped, alone on the side, in the grass, and each time she jumped we saw a little baby hare, as big as a fist, suspended from one of her nipples, but who was not letting go of the goods. There was an old deer, noble and hard eyed like a man who was covered with lichen because he lived in the high fields of Durbonas.

There were bats from caverns that flew over this mass of beasts. And they flew in leaps, deploying their great, hairy skin, and they had legs with hooks like grasshoppers. They fell down and one heard them cry with the voices of young women. There were heavy crows, seemingly weighed down by the night, who swam above the storm.

Upon coming into the village the wolf lay down on the step of the Café du Centre. With his thick red tongue he licked his paws that had been wounded by the needles.

I watched the beasts come.

Soon the rain and the night came. The rain, hard and tight, was enough to make us believe that it was chunks of sky falling upon us. The night, and then, this abomination which filled me broke out all around me like a sun.

I danced that night, with François' horse, and I kissed her on her mouth with her yellow teeth, and, I tell you, I still have a taste of chewed grain on my tongue. I saw men going to the beasts with outstretched hands. I felt that someone was touching me. I put out a hand. I felt hair, I felt higher and I understood that it was the deer. He saw that I was a man; he turned towards my left, and there was Rosine, the daughter of the forest warden.

And there on the Oches hillside, the earth was white with sheep and the big rams were in front, and all of that wool illuminated the night like moonlight.

Then came a beautiful lightening flash which remained suspended in the sky like a lamp.

+ + +

We woke up in a village sweating all sorts of juices, which stank like a rotten melon. I was wallowing in horse manure; a little farther on there was big Amélie, as if dead, her skirt in the air, her undergarments off, showing all that she had.

But, we did not know all of our misfortune until later. Already we knew that Anaïs had a smell about her which would not leave and which eventually drove her crazy. François' horse died of some new disease. It was lodged in the stomach; we opened it up to see. She had a big ball of blood all alive which we stifled under a pile of manure. Finally, Rosine gave birth. What she produced we drowned at night in the torrent, and the midwife of Aspres remained sick for six months. "I still have it before my eyes," she said.

The man had gone off towards Provence. He arrived there by the northern route down the Sisteron corridor. We learned about it from a hired man who came to rent from the Chauvines. A few days later, the man was tending sheep on the Ribiers slope. One morning he was sleeping on the grass when he heard a little noise among the herd. He lifted his head. He saw a man with a bird on his shoulder by the fences. The man was speaking to the sheep in a sheep's voice.

"I," he told us, "when I saw that, I huddled down under my coat and I did not move."

Yes, the man went off into Provence and the heaps of clouds followed him. Then the weather became clear again. But I have a cousin who lives on the slopes of Lure, who told me...

Fields

I often stopped before that wild garden. It was in the most silent fold of the hills.

The pointed roof of the stronghold hardly surpassed the underbrush. An immense black ivy, having gone through the door, swelled its stubborn muscles between the walls. Its hair, filled with lizards, overwhelmed the windows. The crossbar was of dry nettles and covered over with thistles. All around the wild hair of the undergrowth was waving and there was the strong odor of the hostile earth, which had a life of its own, and was independent, like a beast with cruel teeth.

Mute sighs, donning the veil, the color of nervous sprouts of grass, so the entire hillside sang the bitter harmony of despair; it seemed to me, each time, that the terrible bawling of a god was going to surge out of it.

The seasonal rains obliged me to remain in the kind olive groves at the edge of the town; I made use of the good weather one day to plunge into that air above the hillsides.

The stronghold was now clean. The ivy dead; its trunks burned slowly in a brushfire. At a dry clacking of pruning shears, I turned my head: a man was cutting the laurels.

I called out and asked for water.

"My good man. I can hardly give you water; I barely have a finger's worth up there in the old abandoned cistern that I opened, and it is still thick and green and would not agree with you. But, if you would please pass me that wicket of brambles and set yourself down a moment, then I will go find you some grapes."

His mouth, one would have said that it was blossoming with the stalk of hyssop that he was chewing.

The man was made for this land.

He had golden eyes, very soft, a big beard which curled up in black balls; the little pear tree agonizing in the middle of the underbrush still had two leaves the color of his eyes.

I returned many times to see him.

With strokes of the spade and aided by an old fire he had pushed the undergrowth back to the other side of the valley. The land that had been opened up was then ready to receive the seeds of love. It seemed that in this clean space he had, with his heavy feet, danced the dance of order.

In the spring there was a last battle between the man and the undergrowth. The undergrowth had surreptitiously prepared its attack by the slow infiltration of feelers and the flight of blond seeds. One morning he found his land covered with insolent asparagus, gnarled and shiny, and he understood that it was time to settle the score once and for all. Despite the precocious heat, the battle lasted all day long. It was already night when he stood up again and wiped his forehead. Nonetheless he was the victor. And I understood, the next day, that he had achieved a victory over this savage land which he wanted to be definitive, judging from the ferocious way that he had decimated the young oaks and pushed the waves of fire into the very prickly heart of the woods.

The hard sky, the hill, the stifling sun, were of an unheard of cruelty, he told me:

"I do not want to work today, I do not feel well, stay with me a while. Stay until evening."

It was the first time that he had desired my presence.

Then, without transition:

"I am from the Alps: Saint-Auban-d'Oze. A beautiful land! At the bottom of the valley the road stretches between two lines of poplars. On Sunday, girls pass by on their way to the dance, on bicycle, with the handlebars loaded with red and yellow dahlias. At night we sleep to the great rushing of the torrent.

"My house is the last one in the village, on the side of Gap. It is calm; there are no bars across from it. But the long-faced procession of penitents never comes that far on holidays; when they dance under the nut tree in the square I cannot hear the music, and, well, perhaps it is too calm.

"What I have just told you, I understood it after the fact. But, let us sit under the laurel tree."

"In the summer, I harnessed the mule, and we went into 'the land'—a little pointed piece with three willows. You cannot know; there is nothing more beautiful in all the world than the poplars of that region in the morning sun and the wind. I was seated in the front of the carriage, my wife behind. When I turned towards her, she laughed at me.

"Upon arriving, I cut the dry branches and we made a bed for Guitte, I did not tell you: a beautiful little girl that we had, fat, pink, with hips…"

He stopped.

"When one is so happy, one should be distrustful; only, there you go, one never notices it at the time.

"I had my suspicions, like everyone, but I did not have strong desires. I had a few dollars on the side at the 'Credit.' I wanted to buy a carriage, that was my idea. After seeing my wife shaken on a bad seat I got the desire to place her on the slightly more delicate cushions of a carriage. That, too, was not a strong desire."

"Then came the year when the torrent swelled. It ate up not a little bit of land and the commune had the idea of constructing a levee against the strongest arm of the water."

"It was a businessman from Couni who got the assignment, he brought in masons from the piedmont."

"Saint-Auban is not a big village: twenty houses lost in the chestnut trees. A traveler passes through every ten years. There is not even an inn."

"This idea of the tilbury stuck with me. I said to my wife:

"'If we took a lodger? Where two eat, three could eat. A few more cabbages in the soup…'

"She agreed.

"The man who presented himself was named Djouanin du Canavèse. A big man, like everyone who comes 'from there.' He wore large blue breeches, colored shirts, a hat with a large brim set tilted on his curly hair."

"I had met him a couple of times at the tobacconist's shop. He agreed with me. He did not get drunk. When he laughed you felt that you were about to laugh with him. He walked slowly as if his espadrilles were very heavy. In town, they called him: the prefect. I am explaining it poorly, but I cannot even tell you the color of his eyes (yet his stay lasted six months). Beside him I was happy, I never knew why."

"He paid up every Saturday, completely. Once he said:

"'Boss, I put forty cents extra in my payment, for you to buy a shawl for the lady; she makes good soup.'"

"On the fourth of June, we celebrated our daughter's birthday. I had waited for the peddler on the street and bought a headdress with blue ribbons on it. She was a brunette. Djouainin arrived with a bone rattle, a box of sugar plums, and a hidden bottle of wine.

"That was the night that I began to suffer."

He looked at the sun, then the western end of the hill:

"It is time," he said, "if you want to get home before nightfall."

Two days later I saw that the great brambles had cast on the clean ground a thick tentacle of scaly leaves. I thought that I would find the man with his spade. He was sitting under the laurel tree.

"I was waiting for you!"

And with the same suddenness as the previous day he continued his account. There was a great crack inside him, through which the memories flowed.

"...Guitte did not want to sleep. Seated on her high chair she played at tapping the table with her spoon. We had drunk a bottle. My wife said:

"'Djouanin, sing us a little of the song of the lark.' Then as he got up: 'Wait so that we can see you.' And she raised the shade on her side.

"It was a song from the piedmont. His voice gave me goose-bumps; the little girl stayed calm.

"I told you the other day that I did not know the color of his eyes. That was true. Even this time, I saw him without looking closely at him. I was in shadow. I thought: 'One would say that you have been removed from this room.' Truly there was only Djouanin standing in the light, my wife drinking him in with her eyes, and my baby all taken with it holding up her spoon in the air.

"Have you ever received knife thrusts? Excuse me. I am asking you so as to be able to explain what I felt like that morning where, the carriage going as usual along the poplars, I turned towards my wife and I saw her dreamy-eyed, looking at the peaks of the mountains singing the song of the lark.

"At first there was no pain. I only felt something going out of me, leaving a great cold in its place. The suffering came during the afternoon.

"Coming into the house, I went straight to the bedroom and I opened the drawer of the bureau. The box of sugared plums was there. On the cover was the name of a grocer in Gap, and, in the box, my wife had set her little Sunday kerchiefs and a washing pin...

"But under the kerchiefs was a white rose drying, and I knew in all the land that there was only one white rose bush: in the villa of Oze, by the yard of Djouanin."

"Oh! I had become very sensitive. One of my grandfathers, blind, still pruned his vines. By nothing but touch, he distinguished the budding leaf from the budding fruit."

"In the afternoon, I got the idea that the box had come from Gap, and the bottles, and the bone rattle. How could he have known that that was the very evening we were going to celebrate Guitte's birthday? And, above all, several days before? For there is a good stretch of road between Saint-Auban and Gap.

"Then the forty cents for the shawl? And all of the other things which one cannot mention but which a husband knows well."

"On Sunday my wife sat before the door with the neighbors. Beside them I sharpened my scythe or wove baskets. Djouanin played boules."

"'The prefect!'
"He had defied the best players, and the cries, and the 'porca madona!' but he won. When the game was in its last round he threw the ball near in order to draw close to us."

"He was always on the side where the shades were raised."

"I still had Guitte to myself. With us it is said that girls are made with the blood of the father. I needed smiles. The poor girl gave them to me."

"I will make it quick because I am not yet cured of that suffering. He knew how to find the games and the ticklings that were necessary. The little girl stretched out her arms towards him and cried when I wanted to keep her in my arms. I do not hold it against her, it was such a small thing."

"I often thought of that moment where from my shadow I saw him, him alone, in full sunlight, in my own house."

"The first cold spells arrived, I went alone out to the land. Alone the entire day long, you understand?"

"One evening at the moment of crossing the threshold, I heard them talking. One would have said that the voices laughed by themselves. I knew! Upon entering you will find them calm; she will be cooking, he will be on a chair, because it is the time when you are supposed to arrive.

"I gently withdrew my foot from on top of the stone, set down my spade, and took the road to Gap."

"I walked for a long time at a good clip, and all that I recall was the sound that the dead leaves made around me."

"At dawn, I waited on the side of the road for the mail couch. At eight o'clock I was in Gap. I entered the 'Credit.' There were five hundred francs under my name: I took two hundred and said to the cashier: 'My wife will come and get the rest.' He had me sign an authorization. I asked if they could write to her that the money was there for her. He promised to do what was necessary. That calmed me. The harvest, you know, is hard to sell, and, if one does not have a little money for the winter...

"A train was leaving at eleven o'clock; I was at the ticket window in the station behind a business traveler, a comical man who asked for a ticket for Aix: 14 francs 55 cents. I got a ticket for Aix as well. It was easier, I knew the price, didn't I?"

"I assure you that during the entire trip I did not think of a thing. I looked out through the doorway, I listened to the names of the stations, the funny names that you have around here: Oraison, Villeneuve, Volx. After Volx you pass through a barrier of hills. At a certain place where the narrow entrance to a black valley of pines opens out I had the desire to go to sleep there, alone."

"I got off at the next station. But I did not know how to find that valley that I had seen from the train. I climbed up into the hills and I came here."

He displayed the immobile waves of the undergrowth, on the other side of his own land; and above all I saw the great scaly tentacle that the brambles had cast. It seemed to have crept a little more across the turf.

Another day he said to me:
"Give me a little tobacco."
The big brambles were extended all the way across the onion patch. A hardy clematis pointed a green arrow towards the pear tree which the wind caused to tremble.
I left him the entire packet.
And when I came back a week later, the door was closed. The

underbrush blew gently, like an enormous beast shaking. His violets on the threshold were dying. Two or three irises, of the kind which are well adapted to life in the wild, were blossoming despite the mute hostility of the woods.

One morning, by the post office, I was waiting for the country postman, the one who served his section of town.

"I recall," he responded, "three weeks ago (which was about the time that the man had begun confiding in me) he gave me a letter addressed to Italy, even though I did not know the precise tariff. After that, he came every day to meet me awaiting a response. He had promised to give me the stamps, my little daughter collects them. The response did not come. I have not seen him since.

His land, now, disappears under the trickle of woods: a disorder of thistles and wild vines. The pear tree is no longer anything but a dead trunk which supports a heavy, ruffled clematis.

Did he return alive to all of that pain with his soul filled with thorns? Or did he go to sleep, very comfortably, under the savage foliation, and allow his humid body to bring forth this large, creamy, and bitter milk-wort.

Ivan Ivanovitch Kossiakoff

"Let him through: 'Giono to the captain.'"

Night. Rain. The entire company splashing, climbing towards reserve positions on the other side of the canal.

"Let him through: 'Giono to the captain.'"
With difficulty I draw myself from the rank and file where mechanical effort is less painful. In the passage I hear Maroi whining.
"Once again funny face is going to have the best trigger over there."
At the head of the column someone mutters in the shadows before me. It is the cyclist. He's on foot.
"The captain?"
"Down there."
He indicates the rain, the night.
"It was you who made the connection with the English in the Zouavian woods?"
"Yes, Captain."
"Good, you will go to Fort Pompelle with the Russians for the signaling."

"I do not know Russian, Captain."

"What the hell?... They will tell you at the canal."

(I wonder if he means the right path to follow or a method for learning Russian in five minutes."

"Fine, Captain."

"Every eight days Gunz will relieve you."

The communication trench, they told me, ascended straight ahead. It was still raining. No shells. No sound. Calm sector.

A little pine woods without branches. A shell had eviscerated the trench. I hurry. My sack weighs me down, my rifle clings to me. I might have a long way to go like this.

At last the fort, the dirt stairs, then the pit. I inhale deeply. I walk through the grass swollen with water. A thin ray of light reveals the door. I did not see any sentinels, fortunately. What would I have said?

But when the leaf of the door was pushed there was one. Long, hooded coat, helmet: he is unarmed—it works—he makes a sign for me to stop.

"Comrade Rousky, Franzous" (which is all the Russian that I know.)

The man turns towards the back of the corridor lit by a storm lantern and mutters gibberish. There is a stairway which would not sully the manor of Lady Macbeth. There are footsteps above us. I make a gesture to unbuckle my sack; I have chafed shoulders. The extended arm of the sentinel stops me.

"Me, here, stay, signaling."

He does not understand (this is going to be laughable). We go down the stairs.

The one who arrives is a fat little young man. Pink-faced like a woman, well-traced lips. He has on a grey shirt correctly arranged, and a belt buckled around his waist.

"What is it?" he says.

(Ah, a friend, he speaks French.)

But the sentinel rectifies the situation, salutes and speaks. It must be an officer.

Finally:

"What have you come here to do?"

"6th company of the 140th for the optical signaling...(just who is this officer, he does not have any braids.)

"Ah! The French liaison from the reserve, very good, very good, I have been forewarned. I was the one who asked for you. You know Morse code?"

"Yes, Monsieur."

(It came out suddenly without reflection.)

And he does not laugh; it seems natural to him.

"Follow me. Leave your sack, they will carry it for you."

The sentinel disappears. We ascend the Macbeth staircase. A black and narrow corridor. I follow. There is a steel door, that opens with a heavy scraping, then there is a gust of stifling air. Here things are lit with electricity. In the basement the electrogenerator unit beats like a heart. After two detours—(I should have brought my sack, they are going to steal my razor)—the groaning of an accordion greets us. The man-woman opens a casemate. At first tobacco smoke and the accordion—from the ceiling hangs a rudimentary oil lamp—then, silence and in the middle of a blue cloud a little silhouette rises along with an enormous one, broad and tall.

"Enter," says my guide.

He introduces me.

"Your two comrades: Vassili Borrissenko"—(the musician: emaciated; Chinese mustache with cat's skin), then a finger extended towards the tall shadow—"Ivan Ivanovitch Kossiakoff."

Wristwatch, three o'clock in the morning: I arrived at the fort at eleven o'clock. Ten times the thin man began the same refrain again and again on his accordion. His head hanging, he sings: "Vagonitika, soldati, garanochispiat." Is he going to let me sleep?

"There is your bed," says the man-woman.

He should have warned Vassili that I do not sleep to music.

"The rafters, Vaseline, have had enough."

He looks at me, and he continues. Vassili, he is not pretty.

I doze. Music. The flash of a dream: the cat's mustache. I walk in an immense accordion. A green light: Vassili's eye. Pain on my right side: the iron of the bed. I turn over. Music. A drop of sleep. A blade of dream: "It is again the funny face who will have the best trigger." The sentinel must have stolen my razor. Bawling of the accordion: Vagonitika…

Ah! The dreadful night.

Then peace—it is a very soft morning in the trenches. The almond trees are blossoming and my feet are caught in a root of couch grass. I pull. It resists. I pull. The sky blackens. I pull. My head hums…

The casemate, the candle end, but no more music. Vassili is asleep and the colossus pulls my leg to wake me.

"Ay yah! What is it?"

Wristwatch. It is seven o'clock in the morning. Already.

Kossiakoff indicates my signal lantern then the door and he speaks.

"I do not understand, old chap. Yes, the connection. I am going."

I get up.

Kossiakoff seems to be a good guy. They carved his features like scythe stokes on an old elm tree. But he has a wide smile which illuminates his entire face. He speaks, he speaks.

(How do you say I do not understand in Russian? The man-woman told me last night; let's try.)

"*Ne po ni maïo?*"

That's it. The wash of words stops, and Kossiakoff is astonished.

"Yes old chap, there is nothing to be done."

He makes a gesture to indicate that he does not understand either, then a great silent laugh: "It means nothing." We leave.

The signal post is a little narrow hut with squared portholes. Kossiakoff sits down. The skylight which he lets me occupy frames a piece of dirty fog; in the back, barely sketched, the phantoms of trees, the canal. I do not know where to hang my lantern. With his finger Kossiakoff indicates a tree branch stuck in the ground before me.

"The marking."

By chance I send a long ray of light in that direction... Miracle. They respond. A little red glow under the trees. A silent dialogue begins:

"Artillery?"

"Yes. Connection at seven o'clock in the morning; in the evening, ordinary code."

"Understood... Nothing to signal."

"Understood... End of the transmission."

And look. It works. I am very proud. Kossiakoff laughs.

+ + +

I sleep a lot in the barracks. Opening my eyes I find Kossiakoff in a corner, legs folded, head on his knees. He is looking at me. He has given me the entire place. He has made himself small so as to allow me to sleep at my leisure. I am confused. I want to thank him and make him understand that I am not normally the type who sleeps on duty.

"I am tired old chap... Last night Champfleury, you understand Champfleury? Vassili (I imitate an imaginary person playing the accordion), Vassili zon zon zon all night long... No sleep (I indicate my head) badly, tired, understand?"

"*Ne po ni maïo.*"

He has remained folded in his corner. He makes a gesture for me to take his hooded cloak and cover myself with it.

✦ ✦ ✦

The afternoon goes by quickly. I have a letter and three pipes. I read the Bible a little. (My sack arrived intact. They did not touch my razor.) Vassili sleeps, concealed under his grey covering. He does not make any more noise than a bird. At four o'clock we go to attract the artillery's attention.

Kossiakoff absolutely insists on holding my lantern. I walk with my arms swinging, like a bourgeois, behind him; from time to time he looks back joyfully. I feel myself attracted to this big boy who no longer speaks but who tries everything to make me happy and lets his high shoulders carry my baggage.

The front lines are a little on edge. There is a lot of confusion. In the courtyard, under the signal post, a stretcher-bearer rushes by. A battery by the canal begins firing. Here's the response: a grinding cluster of shells fans out over our heads—and is destroyed in flames and thunder along the canal. One by one all of the French and Russian batteries illuminate themselves. Towards the underground shelter where my company is gathered, little black grains scurry about... Friends... Short whistlings and blows of a club. I lower my head, trembling a little in the legs. A shell explodes on the parapet across from us.

I verify the direction with the lantern. Kossiakoff is at his post, jaw protruding, teeth clenched, nostrils open. He is breathing deeply. I watch him. A furtive glance towards me.

"Niett caracho," he says between his teeth.

"How's it going, old chap?"

A second shell farther on. Pieces fall on our wooden roof. "Once again funny face is going to have the best trigger." Another quite near. A rumbling strike passes by.

There in the trees, the illuminated letters.

Pencil, what is happening?

I respond: A.S. Attendez;* I am going out for instructions. I open the door. The talus, like a recently awoken dragon, blows a breath of flame, of stone, and of fine stone debris at me. A thought enlightens me: "Got him right in the belly." The swarm of steel squeals around me "You are going to get it." I roll into the back of the hut and onto Kossiakoff.

I hear him say:

"*Niett caracho.*"

A grey ball comes upon us. It is the man-woman. He is covered with dust.

"The artillery has asked me what is happening, Monsieur."

"Nothing." (The man-woman smiles.) "Respond quickly and do not stay here."

He says a few more words to Kossiakoff and leaves like an arrow.

---

* Attendez = the polite command form of wait

Besides, things seem to be building up. A few more strikes, far away, towards the pine woods. One by one our batteries silence themselves. There is a magnificent sunset in the fog with a cloud rearing like a colt. Kossiakoff gives me two vigorous taps on the shoulder. Take up the lanterns and go back arm in arm. Yes, if you want, old chap.

Upon coming in we wake up Vassili. This damned fellow has slept through the entire alert. He stands up, stretches, and yawns. He mutters something against Kossiakoff who tells him about the whole adventure—I suppose—with powerful wavings of his arms. I amble into a shady corner.

"Shoot. Again the piano with straps."

And the Vagonitika begins. Vassili drinks in the grumblings of the accordion with his cat's eyes like embers; ecstatic, he leans his head all the way down to the keyboard which his fingers pulverize. Nothing else exists around him, not Kossiakoff who taps his boot to the cadence, nor myself who yawns like a sheep, nor all this leprous earth pockmarked with sores upon which flows the harvest of young men.

+ + +

Vassili goes to look for tea. I think that in going to the kitchen I will be able to get some from the man who serves it, and mix it with my tobacco.

He comes back and begins playing the accordion again.

Eleven o'clock. Still Vagonitika with some little variations steeped in a heavy gloom like the wind over the swamps. Is it going to go on like last night? It looks that way. Kossiakoff, almost asleep, looks at me; I see his eyes flash in the shadows. I would rather go to sleep out in the corridor: straw mattress, covers, I move out; and

Vassili, tireless, stretches his melodymaker like a seller of caramel candy paste.

The music stops. I hear Kossiakoff's voice scolding, slightly singing with words that blow like whiplashes. Vassili responds—magpies calling on mountain slopes—the light fluting of sharp notes to occupy the fingers during the discussion. Kossiakoff provides the bass. The last sigh of the accordion. The door opens. Kossiakoff. I am in shadow.

"Hep."

He calls me

"What do you want?"

A step towards me; the light strikes his back. I see his big arms open and close several times, imitating Vassili harnessed to his dream.

"Niett zon, zon, zon, niett."

And he makes a sign for me to return to the calmed casemate.

+ + +

Afternoon reveries on the slopes of the fort. Grey sun through grey clouds. In a blue patch of sky the flakes of shrapnel search for an invisible target. Flat calm. A cyclist, walking his bicycle, passes unhurriedly along the slope of the canal. The little wind with sharp teeth dances in the thin yellow grasses. A sentence by Spinoza haunts me: "Love is an outgrowth of ourselves…" I find it at all the turns of my thought, like that ironic poster towards which the network of trenches always brings me back when I am lost in the Zouavian woods.

In my meanderings in the woods I had entered to escape a low-flying plane, I encountered some friends on repair duty.

"How's it going Giono?"

"Eh, funny face, how's it going?

"They gave you a good one the other day, didn't they."

I shook a couple of hands. I shook the hand of Devedeux, a good sort, a pimp I think in civilian life (he hides his great bangs under his hood and reveals them when he goes to the canteen). I shook hands with Decorde, a café-concert artist, bloated, adipose, and who outlines his eyelashes with match cinders. I hailed him as he turned—always the last one—the caboose. "You will say to Gunz that he should not bother; I am a volunteer for this post; let the captain know it."

I thought about it: here there is Kossiakoff.

Tonight, there is something vexing his soul. He snorts in the stinking casemate as if to seize a nostalgic whiff of desert grass. I bet that he would happily hear a little tune on the accordion, but his companion, once night falls, goes out with his instrument. We are alone. I know the words that must be spoken to calm this heavy pain of a man stooped under the yoke, but in French, alas!

And Kossiakoff leads me under the lamp; from his shirt he takes out a little worn wallet, crumbly, with folded corners, and he spreads it out on the table. A photo: a little round and wrinkled face, a winter apple under an otterskin hat, sharp eyes, slightly dreamy.

I ask:

"Papa?"

"Da."

He nods. He turns the photo so that it does not gleam under the lamp and looks at it—the photo impassive, distant, he with great sighs.

Another: an older woman with a veil around her cheeks, a bitter fold in the corner of her lips, very deep. What sort of claw carved that out?

"Maman? Mama?"

"Da."

I scarcely recall Kossiakoff's voice: it trembles, he must have had that voice when he was young. There is against me, quite near, the bleeding skin, and I do not know the gesture that is needed to heal the wound.

Another photo: a young lady, glistening hair pulled back, heavy earlobes, low cheeks, two vast oblong eyes in a moon of fat.

That I no longer know: papa, mama, international language, but this one: fiancé, sister? I do not know.

"Who?"

He indicates his father, his mother, then himself, then the young lady; I do not understand. Then he makes as if to take them all into his arms, embracing them, the family. The little kernel around which his entire pulp of memories has crystallized.

It is definitely his sister.

I indicate to him that she is pretty.

He laughs, says a few hurried words, then he shrugs his shoulders, he gestures: "What is the use of it?"

How far am I from him!

I unbutton my vest, and I, too, take out my wallet…an international gesture. We are perhaps a million tonight: Germans, English, Russians, French taking out wallets with photos. And how many similar people consume all the rottenness in the mud that is gorged with fat and blood?

My father: his good eyes, the beard through which I ran my fingers.

"Papa?"

"Da."

Now it is my turn to respond—in Russian—with a frog in my throat and a demon in my eyes.

"Mama?"

"Da." (The look of my mother so far away set on this empty space.)

My cousin.

Kossiakoff the interrogator shows the photo of his sister.

"Niet."

He asks:

"Barichna?"

I repeat: barichna between my teeth without daring to respond yes or no. Then suddenly I recall the Countess of Ségur née Krospotchine…old General Dourakine forgotten on the shelf with the dust, with the barines every five pages; barichna, that must mean mademoiselle; the cousin has too young a face for a madame.

"Da da Barichna."

And we laugh, him, with Russian words that scrape my throat, me thinking about the unknown source of my wisdom.

Every evening now, once the shadows come, Vassili disappears. He does not return until the morning to throw himself on his bed and sleep. What does he do at night? There is no watch to take? That is his habitual pattern.

Kossiakoff is the officer who makes the orders.

I make believe that I am writing a letter. Vassili rummages around and draws gently towards the door. I watch him out of the corner of my eye. He takes the bottle of tea and goes out. I listen; I hear him delicately set the container in a corner; his footsteps fade.

I fold my paper—pen—my cap quickly. I have to know where

Vassili spends his nights. He does not go into the ordinary passageway, but I perceive his silhouette on the underground ramp which descends into the heart of the fort. I walk soundlessly down the slope. Detours, I hurry; Vassili's casual step scrapes the paving stones; a stairway plunges into a hole of darkness after the last electric light. He goes down as if into black water: legs, chest, cat hair. Then nothing. Vassili has disappeared; the sound of his step on the soft soil becomes fainter, is lost, falls silent.

What am I doing? Hmm, I have not really decided.

Finally, let's go.

I walk along a wall to avoid the halo of the lamp and I take a chance on the stairs. Perhaps Vassili's evil eye is surveying me from the depths of those shadows.

On the sides of the stairs is earth, a little humid you could say. A faint light guides me; it is a square of night darker than the shadow with a little star in the middle. And now I hear muted sounds of the accordion: "Vagonitika" or rather something more lugubrious, a quintessence of melancholy, of pain, of irremediable sadness with brief spurts of hatred, furious caprioles in a flat key.

"There must be trouble tonight in Vassili's soul." Quietly I approach the opening—wreckage—I see the irregular breach filled with night.

The smooth ascension of an illuminating shell: the accordion is quiet. I raise my head a little, ah I recognize the place; it is on the side of the fort, facing the Krauts' trenches; it is torn out by shell fire and it is forbidden to come here because of the machine gunners who pepper the area during the day. I see Vassili crouched on two sacks of earth. He presses the accordion against his chest; he is hunched over this box of linen and wood from which his cruel dream flows. The shell falls, a bullet cracks against the wall. Night.

And the melodic moaning goes on. Oh Vassili, cold and mute, I know why, now, you look for solitary corners. I know it because I have watched the famous dream to which you give your heart bit by bit emerge from the waves of music.

And each day friendship draws me closer to Kossiakoff, a fur trapper the man-woman told me; Vassili, a student. That one, nothing can be done, especially since the night I watched him. He is sleeping, or rather, hunched over like some terminal god in the depths of the fort, he dreams a long confused dream.

With Kossiakoff holding me by the hand I run over the sheltered glacis and when I arrive, out of breath, he raises me up on his solid arms and carries me like a child despite my cries. We go to the canal and fish for carp with grenades; at the co-op in the windmill we buy jellies, and we eat them while walking, using our hands as spoons. I smoke Russian tobacco, cigarettes as thick as your finger, rolled in blotting paper. Kossiakoff procured me a shirt like his; he calls me Ivan, and he puffs on my pipe without any great conviction.

In the evenings he writes long letters to my cousin in Russian. Then, he mimes his hopes to me: he is married to her and furs abound: soon he is rich: a big belly, whiskers, a beautiful, thick and heavy vest, and an assortment of children arranged in order of descending height like the fluting of a syringe.

The little man-woman inserts himself in the opening of the door. I keep scraping out the stock of my pipe, but my two companions rise up out of the darkness and stand petrified. Then, without noticing them, he comes to me:

"Monsieur," he says, "you have to go to the artillery observation post. There are convoys at the crest of Fort B. and we do not want to watch them pass by in peace. It is a Russian battery that covers the sector; signal the arrival of the cars to them, and the result of the strike" (all that in a sweet and lisping voice).

I stand up:

"I am going right away, Monsieur, but I have never telephoned your batteries and I'm not sure how it works."

The man-woman makes a gracious gesture. It is a bit like the wing of a dove. And that is to say?...

In the little, rusted metal hut Kossiakoff is very uneasy. He tries two positions before he succeeds in resting his long legs. From a hole in the roof the glances we shoot would appear more deadly than the inescapable arrows of Apollo.

On the horizon is a grey pimple: Fort B. A hump of the gentle hill descends and disappears in the woods.

I take out my binoculars. Everything seems just as dead as it does with the naked eye; on the wavy carpet of earth, a spot moves. Pride from my discovery. I hold my breath.

"Hello, battery?"

"Hello."

At the exit of the woods of B., the head of a convoy. The spot moves slowly towards the fort. Through the opening in the water tank, they must already see the postern of the opposite slope. Let's move on, another difficult task accomplished.

A trail of smoke appears on the crest: two, three, three pale mushrooms; like my own land in the summer when it thunders beyond the hills. The smoke blows in the wind. Through the binoculars I see the spot again; it has stopped; around it three black points are spread. It seems to me that one of them is making for the woods, an illusion; it is so far...

Kossiakoff laughs. That is how it is all day long.

But towards evening Kossiakoff finds something interesting in the sector of the Russian batteries. I have already noticed this yellow splotch which seems to be panting in the wind. It's a field of grain. On the border two reapers hurry to gather in the horses' rations. They came out a little too early; the evening is not yet thick enough to hide them; a little regular flash betrays them. And Kossiakoff rests his hand on the leather box where the telephone sleeps.

I stop him. Why kill? Today we have already wiped out the water tanks. It is beautiful, a reaper in the open. They must cast furtive glances at the fresh shell holes around them. Kossiakoff insists. It is his duty. They told him: anything that moves. He does have his secret pleasure of being a watchdog. So I speak and speak. Kossiakoff yawns while listening to my dead words. An anguish torments me, he does not understand; he does not understand. Yes, he has seen my eyes, his arm falls again, a light smile tugs at his lips. He caresses my knee. No more duty: friendship. Duty yes, but happiness given to a friend is something tender, and I would like to tell him, but I am unable. There are steppes between us. Then I make with my hand the same gesture as the man-woman, a bit like the wing of a dove.

I do not understand right away since the man-woman has such a thin voice.

"What, Monsieur?"

"Your company is moving for good this evening. You will continue service until tomorrow morning's connection. You will rejoin Champfleury. You tell your captain that I am very pleased with you."

I ask:

"You don't think that I could come back?"

"No. The sector will be entirely maintained by our artillery which has moved into position. I thank you Monsieur, farewell."

He shakes my hand.

Before he leaves:

"Would you, Monsieur, tell all that to my comrade Kossiakoff? I can never make him understand my gestures."

He turns towards Kossiakoff fixed at his guard post. He speaks. In the entire length of my friend, only his eyes move. As the words reach him, his glance falls slowly on me.

"There, he knows."

The man-woman presses my hand again then—he shows Kossiakoff still stiff—"You have made yourself an excellent friend there. Ah! The Russians, Monsieur…" He is going to tell me… No, he salutes, turns on his heels, and goes out.

A beautiful morning with larks and a little sun. On the glacis of the fort Easter daisies have bloomed; I had not noticed them before.

Kossiakoff carries my bag. Our walk over the fine gravel is the only sound of the morning with the loud rustling of the larks. His step, my step; his step mingled with mine, mine alone. I turn my head: Kossiakoff stops and plucks an Easter daisy.

He has given me that blond tobacco which I do not like, a packet of tea and a roasted sausage. He did not want to accept anything from me, not even this old steel lighter, which he wanted, but which I slipped into the pocket of his jacket without his seeing.

At the canal there is a Russian sentinel. Kossiakoff parleys: there is nothing to be done; he cannot go beyond the bridge. He unbuckles the bag; he helps me on with it. This is it, I balance it with a heave of my back (these moments are still precise inside me), I give him my hand—even to a Frenchman I would not know what to say at this moment. Kossiakoff seizes me by the shoulders, kisses me lightly on the mouth, then with great strides and without a look back, he turns past the shell depot and disappears.

Dumbstruck, alone, empty, I try to call Kossiakoff and the name sticks in my throat.

A hunting plane in the depths of the sky buzzes like a bee.

I went to knock on the little door of the windmill.

"A bottle of Banyuls, if you please."

And I drank. Then I went to sleep in the straw.

It is late. Late for my little village in Provence. The bell has just cast to the wind the ten seeds of the nocturnal hour. On the hearth the kettle still chatters a little with the last embers: I relight my extinguished pipe. The tobacco is very good tonight, unctuous, peppered, strong the way I like it; the peaceful smoke curls around the lamp. My bed awaits me, candid and blossoming purple with amazing, freshly washed linens and a great covering warmly doubled with old silk.

Ivan Ivanovitch Kossiakoff was executed at camp Chalons in July 1917.

Manosque 1920.

The Hand

It was morning. When I went out of the town, dawn was hardly a drop of water. All of the fountains could be heard. The first ray of sun, I met it halfway up the hill. And so it is that now, seated on the slope, I hear steps coming down the path. Who is this early riser, who is even earlier than I?

His step is a heavy step, forceful in its solidity and strength, but slow. The man seems to be testing the position of the stones and leaning on them carefully. I hear a stick searching. It is Fidélin the blind man. There he is at the turn; standing there, in all his height, his eyes reflect the sun like pieces of glass. He rests his spade on his shoulder. I call to him from afar, so as not to surprise him.

"I am coming," he says to me.

And, sure enough, he comes, without hurrying, having veered off a little towards the slope.

"Here you are bright and early," I say to him.

"About what time is it?"

"I don't know, maybe four o'clock."

"I thought so." I told him. I told him: "It is now exactly four o'clock my friend," then I thought, "He knows that better than you do," that is what makes me return. Four o'clock! I still have time to make three rounds.

"Are you caring for the olive tree?" I say.

"Yes."

"Who told you that it was later than four o'clock?"

He taps the slope with his cane, then with his hand, and as he sits down with a great cracking of his old bones, he says to me:

"An earthworm."

He continues:

"An earthworm. When they come out it is five o'clock. I need to touch things. Nothing comes into me through my eyes. They are cold. So I touch with my hands."

"You touch it with your hands?" I say. "With your hands, Fidélin, like that? Like when I touch a table or the grass or even faces?"

I look at his large torn hands and the rough man's skin. Tanned hands from the great tannery, cooked hands, lifeless hands, baked hands in a carapace of dead skin like a glove of mud.

"Better!" says Fidélin.

He raises his right hand, he moves it, and then, in a stroke, I see all of the intelligence of his fingers, all the fluctuating disquietude of the palm, all the knowledge of the base of his thumb, all the enormous appetite of this hand that sees.

"Better! You know that I got it when I was young. The day of the procession for Saint-Pancrace. It was warm, it was May around here, everything was sunny and there was the thick steam of the earth, and I followed the saint, with my hat off, at high noon, at the height of the heat. The one who carried the reliquary in front was named Mathurin, he was a woodworker from Observantine Road. At Notre-Dame, I was one of the first people in the church. The cold gripped my head. They put the reliquary down into the crypt: 'Boy, lend a hand,' said Mathurin, 'It is heavy.' I put my shoulder under the reliquary, beside the shoulder of Mathurin, and I helped set the holy corpse down. I said to myself: 'You have something out of sorts in your head.' Below it was black. Since then it has been black. They brought me back up by lending me a hand. They did not say a thing. I did not say a thing; I was dumbstruck. I was young. I remember the last thing that I saw: Mathurin's shoulder, and then a big candle that was weeping, and then the stairway below my feet. My foot stepped on it, and then nothing.

"I stayed for a long time in my chair. They placed me in front of the door. My mother kept saying: 'Look, look, just try.' I tried and still I had a black brain. In the end I gave it up and cried, I left my eyes alone, I said no. Then, and from that moment on, all that was around me said yes to me and I began to see."

I watch this hand in the grass. It touches a sprig of thyme. The big fingers follow the twisted wood then the palm caresses this cheek of flowers.

"I recall the time when I was a young man. My beard grew. Across from our house was a seamstress shop. At four o'clock vespers they allowed the girls to go out into the courtyard by the iron pits, you know, where there is that old wall older than the town. They came up to me. The ladies called over to me: 'Fidéline, Fidélin,' then 'Here is your cane,' then 'You look like Jesus Christ,' but very nicely, leaning against me rubbing, making me smell the openings of their blouses, laughing, telling me, 'Give me your hand' and they put things that were round and warm into my hands, fleshy things that I knew later to be breasts. But there it was in the blouse. Poor me! A young man of twenty without eyes! You understand, Monsieur Jean?"

"I understand Fidélin, I understand that I would have suffered. All that suffering which I avoided. Never again will I complain, Fidélin. I was twenty, and I had my eyes, may the good Lord protect them!"

"No, it's not that. You understand, Monsieur Jean, all the happiness that it gave me? They were not mean. One fine day, one of them came all alone. She said to me: 'It is evening,' then 'you cannot see anymore, but they broke the lamp at the end of the road,' then 'I was the one who broke the lamp with rocks, last night.' I said 'I heard you.' 'Touch,' she said to me. She took my hand and placed it open on her face. 'Touch my eyes,' she told me, 'touch my nose, touch my mouth, touch my chin; you feel how fine my skin is? You feel how it makes a stream there between the cheek and the nose? You feel how round my cheek is, perfectly round, and then there, between my nose and my mouth, this little border with two slopes, and then pass your fingers there, over my lips, you feel how soft they are? And also the design, follow it, and then, you see, I'll kiss your fingers, touch my hair…'—'Yes,' I said, 'you are beautiful.'—'My name is Antonia,' she told me: 'I love you, and you?'"

He stopped speaking. After a moment, he shrugged his shoulders.

"Well, I have to say something to keep myself amused, don't I, Monsieur Jean?"

Annette or A Family Affair

"You must understand," Justin told me, "tomorrow the woman is going to Chausserignes, then..."

"Just that, on a weekday? Isn't it the market day?"

"No, it is for a family affair."

Right away he took on a slightly distant expression which was just enough to leave a corner of his eye watching me. As for me, I know, I had to pretend to have something else on my mind; I watched the clock.

"Well I am leaving, you must have things to get ready."

"Ah! No," said Justin, "stay a little longer; it is barely two o'clock, and besides, it's raining. And besides, sit down. Mélanie, bring us another liter."

We filled our pipes; Justin filled his over the brim so that it would last a long time, then he wet his thumb with saliva and packed down the tobacco by turning his thumb. He lit the very middle and sucked gently.

"Look, I will tell you about this affair... You remember my wife's sister, Rosine? No? You don't remember? A lady, a real little tart, a little bitch, with allthe trimmings, defrosted, there you go… They found her once with Barnabus, you don't recall? That's strange!"

"Tell me, Justin: Barnabus, is that the one you were speaking about, he is at least eighty, well…"

"This is true, this is, look; I thought that you were older. This is true, this is, but it does not mean anything, listen: this Rosine, she had a daughter by her first husband, then this daughter married…"

"Wait a minute, Justin; how do you expect me to remember? That was at least fifty years ago."

He thinks for a moment.

"Ah! Fifty years, at least that; at least, you said it right, but still it is strange, I remember it myself. Maybe it is because we talked about it in the family, and then, I must have seen Rosine's photograph. Yes, that's right, I must have seen her photograph.

So, Bertha, Rosine's daughter marries and she has a daughter."

"Ah! Well, Justin, she has daughters, that she does!"

"Yes she had three, but that does not mean anything, it begins here. They called their daughter Annette. She was one, she was two, two and a half, perhaps even three years old, but at that point my Bertha dies. She wore herself out sewing linens for others, going to the washhouse in the middle of winter, doing praiseworthy housework. She dies. Good. Her husband was one of those, you know, who was a weakling. On top of that, he liked absinthe. Six months later he died too, all burned up inside by drink. Good. So the little girl is all alone. I remember that at that time my wife told me every evening: 'Also, Justin, that little girl is all alone,' and I told her 'Ah! Yes,' and then we would go to sleep. Rosine wrote to her brother, Eugène, who was a locksmith in the village: 'If you could take the little girl in with you…you who have a workshop, you could keep her; as for myself I am remarried and my husband, you know…'

Eugène did not look right or left, he went to fetch the little girl and took her. This Eugène is not a bad sort, he has heart, but he is without strength of character. He kept the young girl for two years. And his wife was always around to whine: 'And she is here and she is there, and it's all because of Rosine, and she wets the bed.' They had a little boy, who, on seeing Annette climb up on Eugène's knees and call him papa, wore himself out crying: 'He is not your father. He is mine.' Finally there were scenes. In the end, after two years he brought the young girl back to her grandmother. She in turn acted as if he were bringing her a dirty handkerchief. She put her in an orphanage.

There it is! Well, the day before yesterday, now that you know, Amélie came back from Chausserignes and she rushed into the house, and went to chat with my wife: hush hush, under wraps. And my wife said, 'That, after all!' So I asked: 'What is it?' She told me: 'The little girl, Annette, is out of the orphanage she has been placed in Chausserignes!'—'Annette? And why did she come out?'—'She's free,' Amélie said to me, 'She is twenty-one.'

So that's it! You see that, why, she is free!

I said to my wife: 'You are going to put on your hat, and then tomorrow you will go down there to see her boss, and you might even bring him a dozen eggs, not the freshest ones, but the ones from the jar. You will go see him, and you will tell him 'This is our niece, well, this is true, we cannot deny it, but with children like that, one never knows what will become of them after they have been brought up in those houses. Well, you are warned. We are not responsible for anything.'

You won't see her doing anything bad and then their coming around and making a claim against us!"

On the Side of the Road

I went to the inn on the side of the road, my friend Baptiste Gaudemar, called "Gonzales." "Sit down," he said and he sat down next to me by the only table. I drew out my pipe, I smoked; I did not say a word. When I go there it is to listen, to learn. And "called Gonzales" goes for a long time without talking. He has a big cocoa-colored hat that is all stretched out, all washed by the year's rains, all powdered with dusts and summer grains. He has a beautiful handkerchief of red silk with green and blue flowers, this handkerchief which he spreads out in front of the sun at times to peer through and to make others look through as well. "Look," he said "look at this thing that you can only see through my handkerchief." You look and you do not see anything. Then he says: "Look at the sun dance: look there, through the battling sky." You look again. Then, this time you see it.

In the open doorway the entire hillside of "Saint-Mère and Saint-André" is sketched and a good bit of the junipered land all gone wild, despite a high pigeon roost which spits out in silence white pigeons pointed like quince seeds.

The eldest daughter "Mia des Roches" passes by with her basket filled with onions and pears. And there, on the tile floor, her last child—the one she had with a carriageman or a woodsman from Saint-Sylvestre—plays with empty spools. Jeanton, this little one is named.

He looks at me. He passes his tongue along his lip.

"Do you want me to pull out your belly?"

He tells me:

"No."

I say:

"You want me to tear off your arm?"

"No."

"You want me to take off your leg?"

"No."

"You want me to cut off your head?"

"No."

"Well then we can't have any fun."

I look at "called Gonzales." He is smoking and caressing his nice handkerchief.

"During the time when I was in Mexico," he begins…because he went to Mexico when he was quite young. He made his trip in his first communion vest. There they were supposed to have him work in a candy shop. But that is another story.

"At that time…"

That is what gave him the nickname Gonzalès. When we saw him return, dry like a carob bean and so thin that we could count all the joints of his bones on him, so that at first we nicknamed him "thirty joints" for that reason. He was in a vest of old, blackened thread; you would not give more than ten cents for the man and the vest, even with a guarantee. But little by little we learned that underneath, what we took for a big clump of bone was, without a doubt, a small purse, and then we called him Gonzalès, for his money.

"As I was getting off a horse, I saw her behind the gate with her hair parted and her big cherry of a mouth. I said to myself: 'You will give her a dab of your handkerchief.'"

Which made us think that besides the purse he also had a box; because he had a nice way of yawning open-mouthed, of unsticking his teeth and he knew how to look bored and get all the attention in the "Café Glacier" just by sitting sideways on one of the benches. Girls began to hover around him. He yawned, then he had a little, sharp gaze under his eyelashes, and he folded up the entire circle of his mouth, "like a tiger" the apothecary said.

"In the wool shed, with the sound of all those windy sluts with mouths as smutty as bishops', a bed, Monsieur Jean, which has its hundred comings and goings on one side and a full eighty on the other, a mattress as thick as a house, and upon it…"

Upon it—I mean to say after having been well-surrounded by the girls around here, in his story, which I know, since he has told it to me twenty times, he loves it, he sucks it, he chews it like baked honey, and so I do not listen any more from the moment he says: "I saw her behind the gate." I know what he is going to say—one perhaps could imagine that he got some money from it, but, in any case, he does not let on a whit because Jean and Anaïs, and Adelinde are involved, he does not move more than a conclusion. And yet, they were pretty girls, and good for keeping one busy.

To the one who had pulled him closer he said:

"As for me, I am at the side of the road, who knows if tomorrow everything will change? Then, I will get up, I will walk on my road without anything holding me back."

He stayed thus yawning, drinking, and saying: "Look through my handkerchief at the whole sky fighting." From time to time, he came into the middle of the square with his compass, he found north, then he turned towards a patch of sky, and he looked at it as if he wanted to move onward with his glance to that place where the sky meets the earth.

He was at the side of the road. As for me, I understand. Do you understand?

You will understand.

In the evening, his wallet flat, he bought with his last pesos this inn on the side of the road. He married that fat, mustached woman who is there by the stove frying pig tripe. He had two children with her: this "Mia des Roches" who is all wild around his body like a colt, and a son, gone off to who knows where?

"Look," he said to me.

I know the end of the story, I do not listen to it, but each time I look and each time it gives me a great blow in my heart because of all that I am wasting by remaining on the side of the road; I look.

He gently takes his left hand out of his vest, he stretches it out before me... He is like some old, very feeble beast, and there on the middle finger he wears a young lady's ring, even more, a young-lady-ring, all gilded with gold like hair, red-stoned, with a grey blue reflection like an eye.

Jofroi de Maussan

I saw Fonse coming; he was utterly overwhelmed at having his mouth without a chew, at having forgotten to turn up his pants, and with his wool belt below his belly. He was getting ahead!

"If you are going far like that..." I told him in passing.

He did not see me, stretching out his old straw limbs in the air. He turns his head. He looks at me. He climbs the slope, he comes to lie down beside me and remains puffing to get his breath. As for me, who knows his malady... Do I? He speaks about it everywhere: in the café, in the fields, at wakes, on every occasion, ever since Monsieur de Digne spoke to him about it. I tell him:

"That is not good for your heart, you know?"

"Ah! With the heart that I have, if it were only that, but something just happened to me..."

It must actually be something... He, who ordinarily looks at events without haste for a good hour before deciding, he is here, utterly lost, flapping his eyelids, as if amazed by his own speed.

"Did you know that I bought Maussan's big orchard? This winter Jofroi came to my house; I brought him into the kitchen; I told him: 'Warm yourself up.' He drank a small glass and then he decided. He told me 'Fonse, I am getting old; my wife is sick, I am too; we don't have any children, it's a big problem. I went to see the notary of Riez and it was almost understood. He showed me the account, I went to see the tax collector and… I tell you it was almost understood. If I put so much in life annuity, it will give me so much income.' Then I told him that it was a good idea, and, after one or two things, we agreed, and I bought Maussan's big orchard. Not the house; he told me: 'Leave me the house, I am used to it, besides it would hurt me, but take all the land, knock down the walls if you want.' Finally I left him a good part so that he could get his sun and a tree or two for his pleasure. You see that I was agreeable and that I paid straight up. He made use of his money, he had his income. We were very happy. Right.

"Have you seen Maussan's orchard? It is all old peach trees; they should have been taken up ten years ago already. Jofroi, for him, a little more or a little less, it still works, but for me, peach trees are not my forte, and then our land is not a land for that; in the end, see it as you will, me, my intention is to sow wheat there, to pull out the trees and grow wheat. It is as good an idea as any, and anyhow, it is nobody's business; I paid, it is my choice, I'll do what I want.

"This morning I said to myself: "The weather is so-so, you have nothing to do, you'll begin taking them out. And, right away I went to Maussan… (Typical Fonse, this phrase. He did not make it to Maussan until three o'clock in the afternoon.)

"…I attached a rope to the biggest branch and I pulled, pulled and it came; it made a sound. Then I was going to pull out the stump; I heard a window open, then Jofroi came out.

"'And what are you doing?' he asked me.

"His face was not itself.

"'You can see,' I replied.

"'Are you are going to do that to all of them?'

"'All of them.'

"I did not see what he was getting at. He went back into the castle, and I saw him come out with his rifle. Not on his shoulder, well in hand, with his right hand on the tumbler, his left hand on the barrels, and he carried it out in front, firmly, and he walked like a crazy man. He was even less himself than before.

"Me, I had attached the rope to the second tree and, seeing Jofroi with the rifle, I asked him laughing:

"'Are you going to go and hunt down your enemies?'

"'I am going to chase away the scoundrel,' he said to me. And he came over to me.

"My arms dropped.

"'You'll leave me the trees,' he said to me.

"'Jofroi...'

"'You will leave them?...'

"He raised his barrels there beneath his shirt, and you know, he was no longer a man. I said to him, without getting mad (his finger was ready):

"'Jofroi don't be childish.'

"He was only able to repeat:

"'You'll leave them, my trees, you'll leave them?...'

"What was there to discuss? I dropped the rope and came down, there you have it.

"Ah! That is all the stuff of a story!

"And what am I going to do now?"

+ + +

We all tried, tried everything; I myself went to see Jofroi. He is like a dog who has sunk his teeth into a piece of meat and does not want to let go.

"They are my trees; I was the one who planted them all; I cannot take this, here, under my own eyes. If he comes back I will shoot him in the belly, and then I will blow my brains out."

"But he paid for it."

"If I had known what it was for, then I would not have sold it."

"Jofroi," I told him, "it is because you kept the house; so you are still here, you see everything; it breaks your heart, it is a slap in the face, I understand, but put yourself in Fonse's place. He bought it, he paid, it is his; he has the right to do what he wants."

"But my trees, my trees. I bought them at the fair at Riez, I did, in '05, the year that Barbe said to me: 'Jofroi we are probably going to have a child and then the big Revaudières fire made her miscarry. These trees, I carried them on my back from Riez; I did it all alone: the holes, carted in the manure; I got up in the night to light the damp straw, so that they would not freeze; at least ten times I made the nicotine remedy and each can went for a hundred francs. Here, look at the leaves, if they are not healthy, I don't know what is. Where will you find trees this old that are still like that? Ah, of course, they hardly bear any more, but we have to be reasonable, after all. You know that old trees are not young; one does not kill everything just because they get old. Then would you have to kill me, me too, just because I am old? Come on, come on, let him think a little, too."

It is difficult to make him understand that it is not the same thing for him as it is for the trees.

Then everyone set upon Fonse. We went to him after supper in a group. They said to me: "You know how to talk, talk to him; we cannot leave things like this."

I said to him:

"Fonse, listen: Jofroi is stubborn; there is nothing to be done, he thinks like a drum you know. You are the only intelligent one in the affair, so show it. Do you know what I advise you to do? We'll arrange everything: you give him back his land, and he gives you back your money, no fees for the deal, as you said, of course, you do not need to be out anything, and then it's over. He is an old man, we cannot leave him like this, maybe two years away from his death, with sorrow. Let us arrange it in this manner."

And Fonse who is the best old fellow in all creation said right away: "Let's do it."

But then there was something else.

✛ ✛ ✛

Jofroi has already deposited everything into the safety deposit box. He no longer has the money. He only has his income.

He is there in the village square; they made Fonse come, everyone is around; there is no gun, there is no risk of anything. We are here to discuss matters.

"Well if you do not have the money," says Fonse, "what do you expect me to say to you? I cannot give you back your land for nothing; I paid, I did."

Jofroi is steadfast. Fonse's reasoning is solid. It is a wall to crack your head against. There is nothing to say.

There is something to be said by Fonse, because he is, as I said, the best man in creation: frank like a healthy pig who will give all of his blood so that he can be eaten.

"Listen Jofroi, I will arrange things even so. You have your income; you need so much to live; your land, since you cannot return the money, let's call it a loan. So. It will be there for you as long as you live, and you can do what you like with the trees."

That seemed like the wisdom of Solomon to us. We all looked on with happy eyes. It was finished. Things were squared away; I even thought that the monument to the dead was not all that bad. We heard magpies singing.

Jofroi does not seem satisfied. He mulls it over and over again. In the end he says:

"That means that even if you loan it to me, it will not be mine any more. It will still be yours. The trees will be yours."

"What do you want me to say?" said Fonse desperately.

And the comedy began.

✦ ✦ ✦

Albéric came, one of the neighbors of Maussan. He was running. He stopped suddenly, whirling his arms, crying out: "Quick, quick, come quick."

We all began to run towards the farm and, while running, Albéric cried to us:

"Jofroi has thrown himself out the window."

No, he had not thrown himself out the window. When we arrived he was up there on the roof of the house, well to the side, the tips of his toes on the zinc of the gutter. He cried:

"Move away so I can jump."

Barbe was there, on her knees in the dust.

"Do not jump Jofroi, do not jump" she cried. "Do not stand there on the edge where the dizziness might get to you, oh, great

God and good Virgin and holy Monsieur le Curé; take him away from there. Do not jump, Jofroi."

"Take her away from there so I can jump."

We are all there, not knowing what to do. Fonse went in to get a mattress from the bed; he set it on the stones of the courtyard just at the place where Jofroi might jump.

"Take it away," cries Jofroi, "take it away so I can jump."

"You are a beast," cries Fonse, "What good will it do you to jump?"

"If I want to jump," responds Jofroi.

"No, no, good mother," says Barbe.

It went on: jump, do not jump; he kept us there for more than an hour. In the end I called out to him:

"Jump and get it over with."

Then he stepped back a bit and asked:

"Who was it that said that?"

"I did," I said, "Yes I did; aren't you done playing the clown up there? Ah, you are making out well on your roof. You are going to break the tiles with your big shoes and break the gutter. That is what you are going to do. And then you will have gotten far. If you are going to jump, then jump and get it over with."

He thought about it, he looked at us, all of us, mute, below, not knowing how it was going to end, all of us with faces raised towards him, so that he must have thought we were a row of eggs in a basket. Then he said:

"No, if that's the way it is, and since you want me to jump, I will not jump. I will hang myself when no one else is around."

He stepped back and went into the open sky of the attic. Barbe got up. Her dress was covered with dust.

✦ ✦ ✦

This afternoon, which was a good one for doing end of winter tasks, everybody was out in the fields, even the children because it was Thursday. Even me, because it brought out so much laughter and so many songs that I said to myself: "It is spring and the almond trees must be in bloom." They were not in bloom, but in the breadth of the whole plain that was planted with naked almond trees, there was at the tops of the branches like a sort of blue and red foam, the swelling of the sap.

So, I went out and along with the others. There were donkeys, and all the dogs, and the mules, and the horses, and there was nothing but neighing, barking, songs, the sounds of water, the calls of girls and galloping because Gaston's donkey escaped.

In the middle of all that we saw Jofroi pass by. He was foolish; he looked as bleak as a notary in a café. He was dragging a long rope.

"And where are you going?" we said to him.

"I am going to hang myself," he said.

Good. We thought of his stay on the roof and we watched him from afar. From afar… He went all the way to Antonin's orchard, he threw the rope over a branch…

Antonin arrived quickly.

"Jofroi, go hang yourself at Ernest's place, go; here is not the place. And besides, the trees are taller there, and then it is on the other side of the pines, you will be more comfortable, no one will see you, go."

Jofroi looked at him with his stormy eyes.

"Antonin, you will never change. When someone asks a favor of you…"

"Go…"

"I'm going."

And he went. We followed him because in our hearts we knew Jofroi's great pain. We knew that it was a truth, this pain; known by and staring at everybody like the sun and the moon, and we boasted about it. But look at how down there at Maussan a long cry went up and it cast itself out over us like a heavy smoke. It was Barbe who was crying. It was old Barbe who, even in her seventies, was still able to cry out with all the strength of her belly to proclaim that her husband was going to go hang himself.

We even ran a little. He had time to pass the cord over, to make the slipknot, to bring over a piece of wood, to climb up, to put his head in the noose, and already the wood was rolling beneath his feet.

We just had to grab him with our arms around his body, raise him up, and hold him, while he, he beat on all our heads with his fists, and he kicked his feet into our stomachs, without speaking because the cord had already choked him a little.

We took him down and laid him out on the slope. He did not say anything, he just breathed. Nobody said anything. The good fun was over. Children were there to press against the huddle, looking between our legs to see Jofroi stretched out. No more songs. We heard the high wind rustle.

Jofroi stands up. He looks at us standing around him. He takes a step and we step back and he goes through. He turns around:

"Race of..." he says between his teeth. "Race... Race of..."

He does not say of what. There are no words to express all of his desperation.

He takes off down the road, and we see Barbe coming to meet him, moaning, running across the ruts like a little dog learning to walk.

✦ ✦ ✦

"At heart," Fonse tells me, "I am the worst off in this story; I gave my ten thousand francs and if something happens it will not be long before they say that I am responsible, you will see.

Now they are all on my side. But once Jofroi hangs himself for good, or drowns himself, who knows what, you will see. I know them, I do, the people around here. I already have scenes at home: my wife, my child, my mother-in-law, everyone, and yet what do you want me to do?"

"Nothing, Fonse, you have done all that you need to, but as for thinking that you are the worst off, no. Think of Jofroi, he is the worst off, believe me, he is not clowning around. You know him. He seriously wants to die, but he thinks about what he would leave behind, and then, he is not sure, he is in limbo. He says to himself: 'If they see me like that, dead, they will be overcome with pity and they will arrange things;' he sees that it is difficult but he is not without hope."

"Are you sure about that?" says Fonse.

I tell him:

"I believe so. Listen. I went to Maussan the other day. You do not go anymore, do you?"

"No, I have not set foot down there, I do not even go in that direction. It is not exactly his rifle that I am afraid of. Of course, that counts for something, but, if it were only that, maybe... No, I do not go in that direction particularly because I am afraid of that. I will tell you: he knows that I have everything going for me, the law, the people's support, even his own support at heart. Well, if he sees me again, he will think that I have decided to make use of all this. He knows that if I make use of all this, he is lost; and who knows what he will do then?"

"Good, but I went after the rains, and then the hot spell; the field is filled with grass like a basin of water. It is up to the middle of the trees. He was there, Jofroi, and upon seeing me he said: 'Look at this misfortune; if it isn't a misfortune to treat the earth like this.' You see that he is bitter; he no longer knows what he is saying. He knows very well that he is the one…"

At this moment Félippe opens the door of the café. He looks at us. He stands with his hand on the door.

"Fonse, Monsieur, Jofroi is dead."

We remain frozen, empty, without a thought, feeling ourselves go pale, feeling ourselves grow cold like a plate taken off the fire.

Then someone said:

"How?"

And we got up with the little willpower that was left us.

"Yes," said Félippe "he is over there stretched out on the road. He is not moving. He is all stiff. I called him from afar, then I made a detour and came quickly."

Jofroi is lying out on the road, but as we arrive beside him, we see that he is alive, quite alive with open eyes.

"And what are you doing there?"

"I want to get run over by automobiles."

Félippe cannot come back.

"You think that it will happen just like that? When they see you from afar they will stop. If you really want to kill yourself, Jofroi, go throw yourself in…"

"Don't say anything to him," said Fonse.

✛ ✛ ✛

Spring came, then went. Summer came, and went, quite slowly, big and heavy with its big mucky feet with the sun weighing down on our heads.

The Maussan orchard is nothing more than a wild field among our domestic lands. Those who are near it need to be wary, it bites with its long tenacious grasses and you have to strike hard with your hoe to get it to let go.

Jofroi, we held him back maybe twenty times, on the edge of Antoine's wells, a well of more than 30 meters about which Antoine said: "Even so, if he did it, where would I get water afterwards?" We pulled him from the little milldam by the stream. He shook himself like a dog and he left. We hid his rifle. We broke a bottle of iodine tincture, and we warned the apothecary not to give him another, nor salt spirits, nor anything. We were there asking ourselves what extraordinary thing he could do: eat nails, to ruin his stomach, poison himself with grass, mushrooms; get a bull to kill him. Who knows? We imagined everything ourselves and ended up losing touch with reality. Fonse, who has never been sick, had indigestion and everyone came on the run, bad indigestion from a melon. He was two fingers away from death. As for me, I said to my wife:

"Listen, the Jarbois have invited us several times to go see them at Barret. We should go for a fortnight with the little one..."

And my wife said:

"It isn't because of Jofroi that you are saying this?"

"No, but..."

At last it was decided that we would leave. The air is good at Barret, plus the Jarbois are very nice, the husband as well as the wife, plus...aren't they Elise?

And I said to Fonse, a Fonse afloat in his pants, a Fonse in full feather like a pigeon, light, light, white like good china and wearing a vest despite the summer; I said to Fonse: "Come on, let's have a drink because in a few days I will have to go. Yes, on business."

And it was just then that they came again to tell us:

"Jofroi is dead."

We said, in all honesty:

"Again?"

But this time it was Martel who announced it, Martel a distant cousin of Jofroi, a believable man.

"This time, it is for good," he said, then, right away, because he knew that we were thinking about it:

"No, he had an attack yesterday at noon and he died during the night. He is dead, quite dead. They dressed him, I kept watch until morning. I am going to the town hall to take care of the formalities, then to the curé, to arrange a time."

Fonse stayed there for a minute, then color came into his cheeks and he said to me quickly:

"Goodbye."

I saw him go into his house. He came out again a little later and he went here and there to speak to the women. Then he covered the door of his coach, harnessed the donkey, he put a big axe on the carriage, a rope, a knife-saw, a scythe, and pulling the donkey by the muzzle, he left in the direction of Maussan.

✝ ✝ ✝

I saw Fonse again tonight. He told me:

"I will leave five or six of those trees. Not for the crop, no, just so that if Jofroi sees me, from wherever he is, he will say: 'That Fonse, you know, if you look closely, he is not a bad man.'"

Philémon

Around Christmas the days are peaceful like fruits set out on straw. The nights are great hard plums of ice; the noontimes wild apricots, bitter and red.

It is the time of olive crops; for once, the cart will be brought up the bad slope of the hill, and you will have to pull the mule by the muzzle to get it to advance.

It is the time of the pig slaughter. The farms are smoking; in the washhouses they have taken away the washing barrel, attached the big kettle to make the water boil, and, when I come back from a walk on the sunny hillside, I run into Philémon.

He says to me:

"I placed an article in the paper. Yes, because we have to let people know that I am not too old this year. Well, you understand…"

I understand; I read the article. It said: "Monsieur Philémon alerts the public that he is still capable of killing pigs for people."

"Ah! You read it. This way they will know that I am still doing the job."

I met Philémon on the sunken path, and it was at nightfall; he had a wooden sheath in which he kept his knife. I recognized right away the odor of pig tripe and blood that he had about him.

"As for me, I don't smell a thing. It is habit. My wife doesn't smell a thing either; maybe it is because I'm with her all night, and her skin has taken on the smell as well. I think that is it. But my daughter is like you. All month there is no way for me to kiss her. She says to me: 'You smell like death.'"

This smell of murder is so strong that he cannot approach the sows or offer them a hand. He waits there by the bench and the basin. The dog comes, smells him, then goes away with its tail between its legs. And from over there he surveys things. If the man moves, if he sneezes, if he puts a hand in his pocket, the dog suddenly howls a long howl which he sends up to the sky, neck extended, muzzle in the air.

Philémon knows all of this; he also knows that the pig is an animal that is quickly worried about very little, and that the dog is going to complicate the affair; so he stands there immobile, in a corner of the courtyard, with his big knife hidden behind his back.

✝ ✝ ✝

"Do you remember the time at Moulières-longues?"

He laughs. I say:

"Don't you want me to remember? I went for a long time without being able to keep myself from thinking about it."

"It was laughable."

"It was not that laughable; you are used to it, you are, but, then me and the others…"

"Because you get ideas and then once they are formed your mind gets stuck. What was it after all? A pig like any other."

"Yes, but just at that very moment."

"Yes, at that moment…the principal, was to kill the pig before he was dead. That makes you laugh? That is how it is. I should not have been there. It was crazy. It was a rush job, you know."

✦ ✦ ✦

That day at Moulières-longues, the daughter was married. First I must tell you two things: Moulières-longues is a very isolated farm, lost in a sort of crater in the hills where everything takes on a great importance because the surrounding view is not pretty but rather scowling. That is the first thing. The second, is that they have a lot of money at Moulières-longues. Father Sube is renowned for it. So, rather than keep his daughter for the land, he has allowed her to climb and has sent her to school in Aix. Blanchette Sube, big and pliant as a switch, pretty face, but, ever since she has kept me at a distance. There she found a son of a professor or a lawyer, or…anyway, blond and like her: well-matched. Two straws. A puff of wind and then nobody.

I was at the wedding because Sube is still a friend of the family. Philémon was there: because he is a fourth cousin. And then people from all around; and the mother of the young man who pinched her dress together and raised it so she could walk cleanly on the grass. There were about thirty of us. All that I know is that in the end, for the last carriage there was only the "couple," father Sube, Philémon, and myself.

"Go ahead and get in the carriage," said Sube; "I will take a look at the pigs and come along."

He entered the stable, he came out almost immediately, crying:

"Philémon, come quick."

The three of us stayed in the carriage.

After a minute the young monsieur asks:

"What are we waiting for?"

As for me, I had already seen Philémon pass by on the run, then come back with his vest and with a basin before entering the stable, he set the basin on the ground, then he took off his starched shirt front.

I said:

"I don't know."

Sube cried out again:

"Chette, bring me the big knife...the table drawer...in the kitchen...quick."

We saw Chette's eyes grow wide.

I handed the reins to the young monsieur.

"Hold the horse a bit, I'm going."

The pig was lying on its side. Sick. Apoplexy. He tried to breath by wagging his mouth like a fish on the grass but it gargled like a stopped drain.

"Give me the knife," said Philémon, "and catch his feet...lie on top of him."

I had on my good clothes but, I knew what to do, I lay down.

"The basin...under the head...higher...someone to stir the blood...do not let go of his feet."

"Blanchette," howled Sube, "are you coming or do I have to come after you?"

Philémon bled the pig. At first the blood blocked the hole like a pea but Philémon drilled with the knife and it pissed red, clear, in a beautiful arc, like an unstopped fountain. With a little heather broom, Blanchette stirred the blood in the basin. She turned her head; she felt like she was going to throw up, but she kept it in her mouth with her little brocaded kerchief. She was almost as white as her dress. I say almost; and if her dress appeared more white it was because right in the middle was a big spot of blood.

"It's nothing," said Sube, slightly calmed because the affair looked like it would work itself out. "We'll stick a pin in, and it won't be seen."

Joselet

Joselet is sitting facing the sunlight.

The sun is descending in full fire. It has illuminated all of the clouds and made the sky bleed onto the woods. It gathers this whole impenetrable forest, it tramples it, it makes a golden juice come out all warm which then flows down the paths. When a bird passes through the sky it leaves a long black trace all wound up like the tendrils on a vine. You hear the bells ring in the village belfries, there behind the hills. You hear the herds coming in along with the people who harvest the last olives in the highlands as they call from orchard to orchard with voices that are like tapping a glass.

"Oh! Joselet," I said to him.

"Oh! Monsieur," he responds without turning his head.

"So, you are watching the sun?"

"So I am, you can see."

Now the sun is in the middle of battling with the belly of a great cloud. It tears it apart with big knife thrusts. Joselet's beard is filled with sun like peach juice. It dapples all around his mouth. He has it full in his eyes and on his cheeks. You want to tell him: "Wipe it off."

"So, you are eating the sun?" I say to him again.

"Ah! Yes, I am eating it up," says Joselet.

Veritably he wipes his mouth with the back of his hand and he swallows his saliva as if he had perfumed it with some great fruit from the sky.

And when there only remained the green day of dusk, and there, in the pines on the slope, a little drop of light all trembling like a pigeon, Joselet explained it to me.

"That," he said to me, "is what I knew before everyone else. You have heard that I am the master of the rain and that I heal burns with saliva alone? You have heard that when someone has shingles and has tried everything and fed up with everything, he comes to see me, and I'll touch the man or the woman just a little at the place on their waist and the malady goes away? I dry myself with a towel, and they burn the towel and it is over with. They must have told you, too, that with a word, if one has a dislocated limb I'll fix it. If you have a love which makes you thrash about, thrash as if you were on a grill, then you come and see me, we'll come to an understanding, I'll give you a big reading of the stars, I'll put my hand slightly behind your head, and then the woman, there she'll be beneath you, right away, in a moment, even if she is frigid. It is understood that I do that for you once, to please you, then afterwards it is your turn to talk. I give you what is necessary, that is my secret, and if you do well with what I say, she cannot resist, she'll come and you'll work things out with her."

I stop him:

"Tell me, Joselet, is it practical?"

"Is it practical? I believe you it is practical!"

"Do you make use of it yourself?"

He turns his big red savage's face fully towards me. He has a silent laugh all white and red under his beard.

"I have used it, but now…"

He imitates with his hand the wing of a bird in flight:

"…it has left me!

"Yes, it has left me, I had it for a time, but I have left everything behind that has to do with lust for women, it annoyed me. It makes you lose your strength. It does not seem to: you get used to it, it is good, it seems to be good. One fine morning you tap your finger against your forehead. It sounds empty. You say: 'Oh! how light I am; oh! how I am walking; oh! how I am jumping!' You are just empty. It has gotten you off track on the inside. As for me, truly I have need of my power. Power and power, the more I have the better it is. So I shut off the tap."

"You made a big sacrifice," I told him.

"Big sacrifice you say? I believe you."

He has a serious look in his yellow eyes then it widens into a smile.

"But it is worth the trouble."

He remains a minute without saying anything. He looks at the big copse, below it, which starts to move with its nocturnal life. Me too, I look at the copse.

"Yes, it is worth the trouble. Sit down. I will explain it to you. The world, you see, is a big machine. There are the wheelworks, and the springs, and the steam which makes the whole thing go. There are wheels with teeth, they make other wheels with teeth turn, and so on, the entire apparatus: the trees, the animals, the stones, us, the sky, the hill, the Durance, the sea, the seas that are in the stars, the mountains of the stars, the animals on the moon, down to the little creatures below, in the depth of the sky, there where there is no earth, nothing but the mud of the sky made with the dust of the earth and the drops of all the seas that revolve. You see it! When one knows that, one knows a lot, but one does not know everything. Because the wheels are contained one within another, so that when one turns the others turn also. The big one moves just a little, the little one makes three revolutions, the smallest one makes twenty revolutions, a slightly bigger one makes only one turn. You understand? So look: you see the big wheel. It moves just a little. You say to yourself: 'The little one is going to make three revolutions.' Up until that moment it is true, but the other one down there which is much farther away, the smallest one there, takes a moment before it makes its twenty turns. Then you say: 'That wheel down there is going to make twenty revolutions.' You watch. You wait, it makes twenty revolutions. So they look at you and say: 'He guessed, do you understand?' He did not guess, no, he knew. Sometimes the movement that goes from one wheel to another wheel over there takes two years, ten years, twenty years; then in advance you know, that is the whole matter, that is why, me, if I wanted to, I could tell you a thousand things that will happen, it is fatal, the good and the bad, without a mistake."

"Joselet, I would rather not know. Let it happen, maybe I turned the big wheel..."

"You have misunderstood: you are not the one who turns the wheel. You are the wheel. You have done this or that: this or that happens to you because of your movement... But that is not the question, and then, you..."

He begins laughing.

"...plus you did not make the big sacrifice, and I would have trouble explaining it to you, you would not come to know, at least…"

"At least until I come to make the big sacrifice? You know Joselet, you tempt me."

"No, for you this is not possible, at least I mean that you would build up strength inside yourself."

"There, Joselet, I am your man. Every morning I do an hour's work with the axe, and then a walk in the hills, and then I eat…"

"Not that sort of strength. That everybody…"

"Well what strength?"

"The strength of the sun. Set yourself there facing the sun. There, in the evening, when it is not too hot. And then, eat it up, eat it up, as much as you can, quickly, quickly, fill yourself up with sun. Then, strength, it's not in our arms. It is in one's head and one knows what life is made of."

The dusk came. Now the sky is peaceful like a field and the olive harvesters are back in their homes, the chimneys emit blue smoke.

"Joselet," I say gently, "Joselet, is it really worth all that: the big sacrifice and then consuming the sun? A man and a woman who love one another, it is simple and they live life. They are the ones who live life. As for me, I love a woman, she loves me. I create life, a child…"

"Yes," says Joselet raising his hand in the air, "yes, but it is the steam that makes you go, it is the wheelworks, it is the wheel. You are the wheel, she is the wheel. And then, there is only Joselet who knows it, only Joselet."

He stands up. Away from the grass he is nothing more than a big man like a vine stock with legs like tendrils, arms like manure, and, on his bird's shoulders, his big head sways like a pumpkin.

131

Sylvie

I can see her from here. She is up there under the olive trees, standing with her left foot planted sideways on the ground to steady her
against the Alpine wind which plays in her skirts. She is making
stockings. She applies herself to it. I see her round neck like that of
little a lamb and that packet of red leaves which is her hair. A hornet watches her in its circular flight. She thinks that she is alone. She
moves her hand a little. She says: "Go away," and the hornet goes.

I heard the bell of her old sheep. They did not give the ram to
her. First, because she is a girl; then, because it is Sylvie; then,
because of the twenty sheep that she has to watch, and there on the
warm slope of this hill it is not necessary to bother with a ram.

I thought: Sylvie is up there. That made me leave my sunny corner and take to the wind. It is a slow wind, flat and sharp like a knife,
and very slow to enter, well set on the scabby terrain and olive trees.
It moves at its own pace, it does its job. It will freeze up tonight.

Yes, I thought: Sylvie is up there. And then…it made me think
of that afternoon when she came back from the city. I arrived
almost on her heels without knowing it. I enter the farm. I see her.

It has been more than five years. She was sitting there alone at the table. She had not taken off either her coat of fine material, nor her satin hat; she held in her little fingers a great bowl steaming with good tea, it smelled like hyssop and boiled fennel. Standing before her, hands on her apron, her mother watched her drink; standing beside her, her father watched her drink while sucking on his pipe. As I entered she looked at me over the bowl without stopping and everyone toward me with eyes that said:

"No noise. She is drinking."

And I stood by the door.

The bowl now on the table, she sighed: "Ah!" glancing at the three of us, and I saw her face.

I said:

"Jean, she is a woman. She is no longer a young maiden" (That is what is said for a girl who is a real girl. You understand what I mean? A supple girl, a beautiful girl, a fresh girl to put it that way). In her mouth, in her regard, in her skin, there were sure signs which could not fool me.

And to myself I repeated, "Sylvie, Sylvie, who would have thought?" And then: "That's life, are you upset?... Are you jealous? That is life; that is the way of the world; that's it, the law. She's a woman; very well, and so?..."

That very day I noticed the signs on her face; a small starlike design there under her eyes, made with folds of her skin; her lips which at times swell in the middle and this swelling spreads along the lips when one goes to kiss her. Her hands also had very visible signs for me who loved them.

She will never know it; and besides, who am I after all?...

Finally, all in all, when I knew that she was staying once more at the "Chussières" and that she had asked for her old clothes, and that she had taken the red off of her lips, I came forward on my large feet.

I say this because I am not bold. You understand that it is forced: always alone with my washing and my beehives, and so used to the ways of the bees that want slow gestures and things filled with precision, this was a rather loud entrance and people believe that I have big feet.

It is not true. I looked at them in the stream. No, they are not big: they are a man's feet, of course, they are narrow in the middle and then all the toes stick out.

So, that's just the thread in the needle, and, jumping from one track to another, we began to talk, no, she began to talk. As for me, I said: "Yes Ma'm, no Ma'm." That's all.

That is how I knew. Ah! It is not pretty. She still believes that it is beautiful, that it was beautiful. And when I ask her: "But why did he do that?" she tells me: "He loved me, you know," and I say: "Yes Ma'm," and inside myself "No Ma'm."

She does not know. She did not have good lessons, lessons of bitches and dogs, and of male and female birds, and of all the simple mixture that forms even these days, the fruit of the world.

She works on her stockings while watching the sheep. Yesterday she told me: "You see when I began, I was still all nervous, and I skipped the links, look! But now I am applying myself, it is all connected, and it's going much better!"

Yes, it's going better: the juice of the sky is flowing through her.

And, as for me, I am here in the grass watching; I am sunk down low in the yellow grasses. She does not see me. She cannot see me. She will never see me.

Me, I see her.

Babeau

I ask her:

"Babeau, was it really right here that Fabre drowned himself?"

She begins laughing, she looks at her sheep; she looks at me and laughs.

"Ah! Monsieur Jean!"

I approach, and, to soften her up, I also begin chatting.

"That was really some idea of his to go uphill to drown himself!"

In fact it was on one of those fanned out slopes which are the source of floods, two fingers away from being the highest spot in the region. There is a great wart of cut grass and on this wart the cadaver of an ancient farm. A beautiful cypress too, near dead walls, and we are below them.

What made me think of asking Babeau about it, was that on my way up I saw the reservoir, a subterranean basin all in shadow. When one leans on the door, because there is a little door which opens out on the water level, nothing but your breathing snorts inside; it seems like you are blowing into a bull's horn. If you stop breathing, you can hear the drops of water which make a "glout glout" sound like a clock.

"…Yes, here, up above," I say again to put Babeau at ease.

She counts in a high voice: "Four, five, six," the links of the stockings that she is knitting. Then:

"Wait, I am at the skipping part; do not make me miss."

I wait. It is a nice day and the sheep are at peace in the pasture.

"Look," says Babeau, "to get back to what you said about Fabre, did you know that I was the one who found him? Ah! I can assure you, it was laughable. It was done like that, with bravado. Ah! I tell you it was so stupid that I could not keep myself from laughing. I was here, where I am now, under the tree. There was a wind that day! And here you got it first and quite badly because it was the first patch of trees around. It made noise, and I said to myself: 'Babeau you are going to go deaf.'

"He was down below cutting little oaks. Suddenly he came up. He came upon me and said: 'You had better go.' I told him: 'Oh! it is not yet four o'clock.' He said to me: 'Not because it is four o'clock, but because if you stay there, you are going to see me die.' 'Ah! Go ahead, die!' I said and I looked away. He was standing in front of me, there, on that pile of rocks, holding himself straight, very calm, freshly shaved, mustache a little in the air, with a healthy cheek like everybody else. 'How stupid you are,' I told him. I looked down at my stockings and heard him leaving. I thought to myself: 'Even so, that man, how stupid he is, how stupid he is! Not bad, he is just stupid!' And then again the sound of the wind in the trees filled my ears, and the needles kept my eyes busy, and that went on; I made a crossing of my hands on the stockings, then from the sun I saw that it was four o'clock, and I called my sheep.

"Coming down, in front of the reservoir, I saw Fabre's hat, and then his vest, and on his vest, his watch. I said: 'He is even stupider than I imagined.' I looked in at the door. By God, there he was lying on the water, all calm. Earlier, he must have beaten the water with his arms and legs because it was all splashed up on the walls and the ceiling, and the moss in back was torn out; there was a big piece of it on the stone. What made me laugh was that above his cheek a little frog had settled. It was terribly frightened! And I had to see that at my age!"

The Sheep

Félippe was going out into his almond trees; I saw him out there where the wind blew, sniffing, nose in the air, looking carefully at the four corners of the sky, and what he saw decided him. It was a wind that wanted to work; something heavy swept in from the sea, with beautiful, thick clouds. That was the state of things.

I came down, I took big steps on the path where Félippe went at his own pace. It is very much Félippe, that slow movement of the legs, that head looking right and left at the same time, that way of carrying the hoe, the steel against the shoulder, the arm pointing out in front; the tool holding itself up by itself, hands free to enjoy the warmth in his pockets. I catch up to him; he says to me:

"I am going to the almond trees; if it rained a little later that would be good. Me, I always arrange to do half of everything."

"How, do you share things with your son-in-law?"

"No, that is not what I mean; I mean that I do everything halfway: a little bit by me, a little bit by the weather. As for me, I am going to dig circles around the bases of the trees; the weather will make the rain. Between the rain and the circles, we will surely manage to have flowers."

"Ah! Yes, like that, I see, but you have not thought of everything; there is not just you and the weather, there is also the tree."

"The tree? I left it out intentionally. I can tell that you are not familiar with them. If I were not here, it would do just as it pleased. The tree is entirely whimsical. It is intelligent, I do not mean, that it understands things…but it is like an animal, it spends its time pleasurably. I will tell you. Do you know where my orchard is? There, at the end of the plain. The cold wind, it hits full-force. Well, since before Christmas, you have noticed that there has been fine weather? Good, very well, you will see. There are two or three that have blossomed; if they were still young, that would work, there would be an excuse, but old ones! And well, they seem to find that fine and good. They do not do it in secret, no, they do it just like that, for glory, to say: you see, look how strong I am! I am out in front. They are like that, you know, trees are. And then, as soon as the mistral begins they will bend as if they were in front of Jesus. The others, with their folded flowers, that will be easy for them; they will rain down on your back because they are like that, this wind, which wants them to rain down on your back, if they do not have flowers, then it is easy for them. These trees, by following their whims, first they freeze, and then comes their pride and joy, these flowers, but they stick out their stiff arms, they want to be showy and that makes them break their branches. I have seen them die of it."

We arrived on the edge of the plain. In the ground there are big fingernail marks from the storms and fresh scars, and there are ravines that are slightly revived with a crust of young trees. I go all the way down to the valley below. I see the tops of the roofs of two villages across from me, one on each side of the torrent, and a bridge. You can see the river with its blue water clearly cut in its bed of stone; and then the fields in the valley which resemble those throw rugs that you make for the foot of beds with pieces of cloth from all the clothes that you no longer wear. You know how they sew the pieces together with big stitches, there are bits of every color, plus bits of velour, canvas, wool, cloth, silk, at times a piece of a nightgown...

"Look, the nightgown," says Félippe to me, "that could be this field, there, I think that it is the field of Bélin de la Bégude. You see it with its little flourishes. My wife had a nightgown like that when she was a little girl."

We walked along the edge of the plateau, then Félippe said:

"I'll show you the sheep."

"A dead sheep?"

"Ah! I don't know if he is dead, but I'll let you see him. Come on, he has to be here."

Here is a promontory that extends its point out over the valley. It presides over all of the lower parts of the hill.

He points his finger.

"Look, you see him there?"

I look: there are small hills and green oaks. I say in good faith: "No, I don't see him." And even though I know my Félippe, I was looking for an actual sheep. There are times like this when one lets oneself get taken in.

"You do not see him? You do not see him there? Look he is lying flat on his belly, his feet folded beneath him. You see there, you see his rear haunch. His tail, it is that great tuft of trees down there by Anatole's farm. You see the sheep? It is an old one: look, above his back, he is all bare; all that is left are those pom-poms of junipers on his flanks, which really seem like wool. You see over there you could say that his front feet are folded. The sheep, he has feet like a folding yardstick, and it folds straight up. And well, then you see there his neck stretched out on the side of the plateau; he is going to hide his head, there in the pine trees. You see him? Doesn't it look just like one?"

"Yes, it looks just like one, it is a hill lying like a tired lamb in the mud from the torrent; his neck extends down towards us, all stretched out; you even look for his head, there under the pines. It is a lamb who extends his four kilometers in length and at least two in width from the valley of Fontenouille to the farm at Garcins."

"You see?" Félippe says to me. "He is not alive, the sheep. He must be dead, as you say."

He remains silent a moment, then:

"Don't contradict me, but it really looks like a sheep doesn't it?"

Then he continues his thought, or perhaps his mind leaps to something else, or perhaps…one never knows with Félippe.

"I brought my knife-saw. You see the fourth tree down there? That is always the whimsical one; I am going to cut a few branches off it, that'll show it that I am the boss."

In the Land of the Tree Cutters

There was an olive tree. Ah! In the valley all soft with greenery there was also a pine alley, a copse of cypress, and, in town, a boulevard under the elms.

Saturnin said to me one day:

"That olive tree, look at her, how pretty she is! Things like that hurt my eyes. The last time, I can't even remember what made me look. Would you like for me to tell you about it today? It makes me think of Africans. You see: little Africans who are not fat, Africans from the countryside with, all of them, full pitchforkloads of straw on their heads. You see: they are going up the hill. They are going up the hill, you see, with their grain; they are on their way to feed some big animal from their country. One of those animals that has thick skins like stones."

The pine alley, set off from a field, ending in the middle of a field, without purpose, like that... But there was in the east a perpetual whisper of wind. It sounded like a beautiful underground stream with its cavernous rumblings. It was fresh, dark, supple.

The cypresses, when one entered the copse, were like a chalice of flowers with a white pistil: a pedestal of old stone all alone which sufficed. And they say, "Long ago it was…"

They cut down everything. Everything. And since the olive tree was troublesome with deep roots, they used petards with black powder to blow them out. They had the last word. Boulevard!

These elms clothe it. You could see, here and there, the old and flaccid skin of the houses and even the disturbing sanies, but beyond the trees, beyond the birds… Ah! The birds. Wait, I'm thinking of them. On summer nights, these elms shelter two owls; they coo a tremolo which makes all the water in your heart shiver. At sixteen they consoled me after a heartbreak.

They cut down the elms; the boulevard is bare. It is there, now, yellow and dirty, all pimpled with a tumor of factories that sweat vapors and thick waters.

All of our entire land passed through the fine shears: the land had just been condemned to forced labor in perpetuity.

✦ ✦ ✦

I went for a walk on the hill with Jérôme, the old shepherd who makes forty cents a day.

"Jérôme," I say to him, "you know a lot of things, do you see that ruin of a farm? And the lovely cypress next to it? I wanted to ask you: in the hills, that tree next to the farm is still standing, do you know why?"

"Ah! My good Monsieur, yes, I know, I will tell you. First of all, this farm, they called it: The Beans because there the earth was good for beans. If you had smelled its perfume in the spring with all that in bloom! And I am going to tell you in general and then in particular about that farm. In general, look: in my day they planted cypresses. Do you know why? Because it is a tree that sings well. That was the reason. They did not have to look very far. They liked the music of the cypresses. It is deep, it is a bit like a fountain, by farms, it flows and flows, it makes its noise, it has its way, it lives, it keeps you company better than ten men and ten women whom we need not mention. Here, we could not afford the luxury of letting the water flow so much, and besides that, here we would measure water by the can. And also, we craved the companionship of things that are not human. As an aside, I'll tell you that, but me, I have thought things over quite a bit in my pasture: he who does not have this craving, make the sign of the cross to him and go on your way; that is someone who is lacking something; his mother made him a miser; he does not make good company. So, to replace the fountain we planted a cypress by the farm, and just like that, in place of the water fountain, they had a fountain of air with just as much companionship, just as much pleasure. The cypress, it was like that stake that you drove into the moist slope to create a flow of water. They stuck the cypress in the air and they had a current of air. They came to sit beneath it, to smoke, to listen. That sound on top of the worries in your head, ah! How fine.

"Now for what is special about this particular cypress, I will tell you; I was a shepherd there, I know about it. We went to get it, Firmin and I, down there at the bottom, you see? It was already a beautiful tree and heavy. It was a lot of trouble to bring it up here. We did that together, Firmin and I, the day that Firmin's wife had her child. What use were we there, and besides that, we couldn't take her cries. We went down, and we both sat down beneath the tree, and push against push and slide against slide and swear against swear, one against the other, and both of us against everything we dragged up there. The little one had just been born. It went well. They had the baptism down below.

"Firmin died. Madelon died. The little one did not come back from the war. The tree remains."

The Great Fence

I just saw one of the great dramas of the earth. I made the necessary gestures. You should understand: not just any, not those of
someone who does not know; the gestures which I learned slowly,
with all the tenderness of my heart, the gestures which crept into
my nerves and my muscles, little by little, by drops you could say,
well-learned, well in my blood, the exact gestures. They were the
poor gestures of a man. I did not believe it. I knew it, because,
despite them, I had been stopped by the great fence.

Ever since I have said: "Even I…"

Ah yes, even I.

+ + +

It was a pretty rain. One of those April annoyances: with great gestures of wind, then the lashings of cold water like the thousand
strokes of a whip, a low sky showing all the swellings of its muscles.

But towards evening I put on my cloak, I took my beret and I went out. In that room filled with pipe smoke, I began to have what seemed to be hallucinations of the bottom of the sea. Two strokes of the wind put me back in order. I see the weather like it is, and I tell myself: "You can climb the hill," and I climb it.

It is that hill over there, round and beautiful and smooth like a breast. But it has a name: hill of Aures, hill of the wind. That is to let you know that I was not seeking shelter.

Towards the summit, the wind and the rain whipped up in swirls that were seen drowning themselves in the trees. A black air flowed with a torrential fury. A shapeless thunder rattled up above like in a giant toad. The olive trees were suffering beautifully. And yet the olive is a hearty plant which has seen pain and disappointment. That is the sum of it.

There was a moment of calm. A great, clear day fell on the countryside like a fisherman's net. In the sky, suddenly depleted of rain but still shivering, a stuttering groan floated by.

It had the effect of a fist in my face. I stopped. I looked. I looked especially in the direction of some high grass where it seemed that the cry was coming from. Two great crows flew up from the grass. I recognized them. They were the old savages of the plateau. The old, hard ones who hunted rats and marmots during winter and who fly in the spring towards our gentler slopes, towards more savory prey.

They rose above the grass, with a simple shrug of their shoulders. Just enough to set themselves in the olive tree.

The groaning began again. The crows watched me. They began crackling like breaking branches. It was a warning. Then, from the grass, a rook flew up. A big rook heavily built, with a soft flight, which caught himself in a shaft of wind, wobbled on its two wings and fell like a wave in the emptiness of the valley. There was no mistaking it: it was a satisfied animal.

The cry again.

I chased away the crows with stone throws. I approached the grass. The cry had stopped. I looked: there was a little shivering of fur which guided me. It was a hare. A magnificent beast in pain and confused. She had just given birth to her little ones, all new. They were two bloody sponges all pockmarked by beak thrusts, torn apart by the bill of the rook. The poor thing. She was lying on her side. She, too, was wounded, her living flesh torn. The pain was visible like a large living thing. It was stuck in that large wound of her belly and you could see it moving inside like a beast wallowing in the mud.

The hare no longer moved.

On my knees beside her, I gently caressed the thick fur burning with fever and especially there on the spine of the neck where caresses are gentlest. All that was left to do was give compassion, it was the only thing left: compassion, an entire heart filled with compassion, to soften, to say to the creature:

"No, you see, someone is suffering from your suffering, you are not alone. I cannot cure you, but I can protect you."

I caressed and the creature did not complain any longer.

And then, looking at the hare in the eyes, I saw that she was not complaining any longer because I was even more terrible to her than the crows.

It was not appeasement that I had brought there, next to this agony, but terror, a terror so great that from that point on it was useless to complain, useless to call for aid. All that remained was to die.

I was a man, and I had killed all hope. The creature died of fright beneath my misunderstood compassion; my caressing hand was even crueler than the beak of the rook.

A great fence separated us.

Yes, at the beginning I said: "And even so, I…" It is not out of conceit, it is out of surprise, it is out of naïveté.

I, someone who knows how to speak the language of the titmouse, and there they are on the stairway of the branches, all the way down to the ground, all the way to my feet; I who the *lagremeuses* approach until they have me painted backwards on the golden globes of their eyes; I whom the foxes watch and then, in a moment, they know who I am and pass by gently; I who do not scare up partridges—they peek without raising their beaks; I who am an animal among them all on the great weight of the hills, the junipers, the thyme, the wild air, the grasses, the sky, the wind, the rain that I have inside me; I who have more compassion for them than for my fellow men, if there was someone for whom the great barrier should fall…

No, it is there. It took our evil accumulated over the centuries to make it this solid.

I believe that these are useful reflections for Easter time.

The Destruction of Paris

I am back from Paris. Yesterday in the night, the little path took me
on. I felt its wet grass on my ankles; the bare branches clung at my
coat. I pushed my door. My mongrel leaped towards my face lap-
ping the air with great strokes of his tongue; my cat jumped on my
shoulder. My cat! My new cat! A strange animal fiery and black, a
tree limb cat, a wild cat that arrived a month ago from beyond the
terrestrial world, through the branches of a tree to me as I walked
in the hills.

There was a beautiful full moon just for me.

I recall that man who I met on the Boulevard St. Germain. He had
just taken a newspaper from a hawker. He had precise gestures for
it. Hand stiff, fingers sharp, a concern for the five cent piece, no
concern for the newspaper, and now he was running along the sidewalk, the paper in his fist. He had a curled-up face, eyes which
looked far ahead but with a sadness and a full weariness in his
mouth. He ran. The run of a city man. I followed him with my

great steps. I said to myself: "He is in a hurry, where is he going? What is his goal?" With a jolt he stopped on a streetcorner. No haste. The end. The goal was there. A streetcorner somewhere. Not even somewhere, next to a cheese merchant; as for myself, accustomed to country smells, I was stifled by that odor of Camembert. I wanted to know the last word. I waited. The man read the newspaper. He was still sad and weary. The bus arrived. With a jump that I did not think him capable of, the man threw himself into it. Through the windows I saw him sit down, look vaguely around, take up his newspaper again. The bus took off at the sound of a bell.

It is for that man that I want to write this evening.

✦ ✦ ✦

Monsieur, my dear friend, man. Man, that's how I'd like to address you, if you'll permit me? Man, do not run any more, do not hurry anymore, I saw your goal. I saw your goal because I have new eyes, because I am like a child, because I understand, like children. Do not run any more, you went the wrong way. I watched you, I saw you; I know how to watch men, and I do not want to believe that the goal towards which you ran was that corner of the sidewalk with the smell of cheeses where the bus stops at a square filled with mud. It was because you looked far away with your sad eyes. Listen to me, I am going to say it gently to you:

You saw, in the evening, that phosphorescent blot of autos that turn around the Place de la Concorde. One might say that something kneads this dough with great blows; it cries, it turns, it does not rise, it does not have any yeast, it turns then it flows like clear water and it will stagnate in the fine depths of houses. All of that, the entire city, all Paris hastens and runs like you towards the goal.

Blind men! You are blind men. Run, you can run: the goal is behind your back. There is no bus for that direction. You have to go on foot. We would have to take you by the hand and say to you: Come, follow me!

Man, listen to me, I am going to take your hand and say to you: Come, follow me. Here I have my vineyard and my vines; my olive trees, and I am going to supervise the oil myself in the old mill all steamed up among the naked men. Have you seen my dog's love? It makes you think, doesn't it? This evening in which I write to you, the sun just set in a striking splashing of blood. The original myth of the death of the sun, I have never read it in books. I read it in the great book, the one around us. I was slightly annoyed yesterday morning because I had three extra pigeons in my pigeonhouse. Three ring pigeons all proud and cooing who came to submit themselves to the seeds in my hand. I have here under my window the fountain of a water that I went looking for with a pickaxe.

That is the goal, that is what you saw with your sad eyes, there in the depths of the air. Come, follow me.

Follow me. There will never be any happiness for you, man, except for the day when you are in the sun standing beside me. Come, tell the good news to those around you. Come, come all of you; there will only be happiness for you the day when the great trees burst up through the streets, when the weight of the wild vines will make the obelisk crumble and bend the Eiffel Tower; when in front of the ticket windows of the Louvre you will not hear anything but the light sound of ripe pods opening and the wild grains falling; the day when wild boars will emerge from subway tunnels wiggling their tails.

Magnetism

I met, en masse, these men charged with great strength. I only had to push the door of the little café run by Antoine...

For a long time I have been coming to this slender mountain village. It is on the outskirts of my land; it is on the border of the mountains, besieged by foxes, boars, forests, and icy waters. The high pastures sleep among the clouds; the sky ebbs and flows beneath the great wind; up there, only the empty grey and the silent flights of eagles like passing shadows remain.

The men who live there are hardly numerous: ten, twenty, call it forty by counting those from the lost hamlets and the travelers, those who enter by one road, take a breather there within the shelter of the houses and leave by the other road. And the earth, all around is wide open. The width of the land, precisely, is terrible, the nudity of the land, the solitude of the land around there. For, you see: ten, twenty, call it forty, that makes only a few men to inhabit all of that. Every day you have to go to work: trapping animals, cutting trees, reaping the harvest in some lost valley; or even, suspended on the grey shoulder of the Garnesier, walking in the warm footsteps of some strange mountain beast made of rocks and clouds.

So there is a lot of sky, a lot of air between these men when they leave the village for their work. What they inhale does not have the odor of having been previously inhaled. The air that they breathe does not come from the gut of other people. It is pure and from the source. It is good on the one hand, but it is bad on the other, given that this purity has to be bought with solitude and desperation.

You, me, and I say me out of politeness, because truly my greatest pride is to have this magnetism which I will tell you about, we would be there, all year, playing our games like they do; a strange fear would take hold of us, no longer daring to dip our full pitcher into the spring or hack a tree with an axe.

I pushed the door of the little café run by Antoine and, all together, I had them there, with me, those men charged with great strength, those men who carry the magnetism of the earth, the men who have steeped too long in the thickness of the sky and who now, are like sponges heavy with sky. The sky is there under their tongue and by merely opening their mouths, out flows the sky with all of its wisdom, so that their breath is cut short.

Ah! Just before coming here, I was with other men—if one can put the same name on a noble animal, my brother, covered with hair, who plays his accordion there, before his bottle of wine and the artifice of over there, so hollow under his beautiful vest that he resounds like a pipe.

And I was saying to myself: If some spasm of the earth, suddenly, made everything but this place cave in, if right now, going out for the "evening" one found the virgin forest at the door, the virgin land, the sky, the wind, the rain all virgin; if everything was lost of of the discoveries and the sciences and art, if we were suddenly back at the beginning, how many true men would there be in there? Of those who know how to select a slope, choose the grass, make traps for meat, walk with the stars, propel themselves by the wind, vanquish the cold, live in the end, to live with all this would demand courage. How many? Maybe you, I say to myself; maybe your friend who is there and who is like you, that would make two. What pride!

Here I pushed the door to the little café run by Antoine, and now that I am here, if I think of the same thing, I see them all, my beautiful men heavy with great strength. I see all of them there heavy with the great magnetism of the earth and the sky going out into a virgin world with the same square shoulders which they just used to open the door and go out into the night of the old world, in their village threatened by foxes, boars, the forests, and the icy waters.

And that is why the morning after, when I met at the gate of the barn the man who twisted the long straw strips and fixed them with the bark of a hazel tree, coiling them in great flats for the chicken feed, that is why I approached him and said:

"Show me. That is good work; show me how it's done."

And in my heart I said:

"Yes, teach me, teach me, tell me what I really want to learn, I beg you. Teach me. If you refuse I will be desperate and naked."

Fear of the Land

Yes! And I told myself: "By living in the thick of the hill that will leave you. Look: it is not the earth that piles up in your shoe; it is a flower; it is the wind; it is the plateau that is used and which cries out under the wind like iron in the mold. What are you afraid of?"

Good. But, summer or winter, the wide-open land is there and I survey it over and over, the wide-open land holds me at its mercy.

I also told myself: "It is in your head. You see what happens to you when you try to get to the bottom of things! Drop all of that, make yourself into pure peacefulness while working the earth for food, like all of those people of the forgotten farms around you, like Jacques, like Clovis, like Hugues, like Sansombre." And, you know, I just saw Sansombre; and he was fighting against this very same fear!

I went down to Reillanne. Not on business, no, but with my hands in my pockets, like that, filled with enthusiasm, because on that very day the plateau wore its malice in full view. I had given a stroke of the hoe in the thick of the garden and underneath were the roots of junipers, as broad as my thigh, and ready for the attack. Usually I pass through that forest; this time I took the road: the road is a little bit of domestic land. There I heard a cane up ahead tapping and I said to myself: "That must be either the postman, or I don't know who." But I did not try to catch up with him; this fear of the land does not give you the desire for company but rather disgust for everything.

I have good legs, and without even trying, I gained on the person up ahead. At a turn I saw him, it was Sansombre. What was he going to do at Reillanne, on a day like this?

This village which I am telling you about is just a twisted road, and, lined up on the road are the grocer, the tobacconist, the post office, the café Fraternité, the Mouranchon sisters' house, and then the sows, and the stables, and then the low windows and behind the windows the old women knitting stockings. After that, the road turns out again on the flat of the round earth.

I spend the morning looking at the houses, breathing in the odor of manure, watching a horse that went by itself to drink at the fountain. And I said to myself: "That, yes, is an animal that matters! If you had that next to you, then you would know what to cling to!" I caressed the horse. He was turned with two legs crossed, and without stopping his drinking he made me see his big troubled eyes, troubled…

I avoided my Sansombre who tried to do the same thing as I did two or three times. He went into the stores. Not to buy anything: he entered, he said: "Hello, well, how's it going?" They responded: "Not bad, and you?" And he responded: "Oh, me!…"

I went to the Fraternité. Well in the back, in the shadow. I asked for some wine. Sansombre also came into the Fraternité; he could not do otherwise. He sat by the window, he had them serve him a bottle of wine. He drank it in full glasses, leaving a little space between each glass, then he asked for a second liter. At one point he looked in my direction, without seeing me; in my shadow, I drank softly and then I set the glass softly on the table without making a sound. He looked in my direction, his eyes were troubled like those of the horse. There was only he and I in the café.

He asked for large coins; and they gave him some for twenty centimes; ten big coins of bronze spread out on the marble. He gathered them up and went over to the player piano.

He played all of the pieces, one after another without stopping, then he began again. He was there, on his chair, squarely poised, his body straight, arms hanging, but his head was tilted to the side on his shoulder like the end of a sick plant. And as for me, I was also like that in my shadow.

The night came. Outside they lit the three oil street lamps: one in the middle of the road, the others at each end. The owner of the café was frying onions in his kitchen. Sansombre left money on the table and left. As for me, I waited a little, then I called "Boss!" She did not respond; I left the amount as well and left.

Sansombre was ahead of me, but I found him at the end of the street, stopped at the edge of the night, just at the frontier of the lanterns and the night. He looked, from there into the depths of shadow of our damned land. I stopped next to him; I began looking, too, for a good while, and then I said:

"Yes, it is over there!"

He turned his big troubled eyes towards me. I understood that he was thinking like me: "And to say that we are going to have to go there!"

Lost Rafts

In a little village of Ventoux, a family of peasants is on trial. The young man strangled his wife. After that he took his dead wife on his shoulders and went out and to hang her like a Guinea hen by the stairs of the barn. The father was eating his cheese under the oak. He saw the son pass by with his charge.

"Where are you going?"

"To hang Augusta."

It seemed entirely natural to him.

That should be rather hard to understand when one is not out in the middle of the land. I say "middle of the land" as they say "middle of the sea." This old Rodolphe who was eating the cheese, he was the captain of all that. If he did not move, if he did not see anything but the ordinary in the weight of the dead woman that his son balanced while crossing the yard, it was because he had prepared everything long before. Augusta was a rich orphan. Before going farther, and explaining everything, you have to know the countryside: the black woods, the red and dark hills, the mute valleys. Once in awhile, a bird passes by. It is a magpie carried by the wind, who fights against the wind to return to his land but who allows himself to go with the flow because, from above, he saw beyond the hills the wide red and green countryside. One has to wait again for another gust of wind before seeing another bird. The land is covered with low oaks. The oak takes a long time to sprout its leaves. It takes a long time to lose them and it keeps them dead on its branches for a long time. There are barely two months of green leaves. The rest of the time there is no voice in the landscape, no song of the trees, only this sound of dry bones and broken stones, when the wind flows in the oak groves. The farm, I know it; attached to the land like some domesticated animal, a back of stone with huge muscles, and, blowing in the black dust of shale, a little head which is like a sow with piglets. Narrow windows, just wide enough to allow the muzzle of a gun to pass through. Inside one has to feel the way with one's feet like in a cave. Stairways everywhere, those which go up and those which go down. They are not the same: some lead to the attics, the others to hidden places in the rock. Down below, in the black belly of the house, there is always a well or a cistern. It is never protected. It yawns with its big humid mouth at the level of the stairs. It remains there. It is a good threat, a good remedy which is there waiting patiently. It could be put to use, maybe by chance, maybe one could help chance a little with an elbow push if one has a wife who produces too many children, a girl who is a little beyond help, or an old father who is lingering.

So, Augusta was a rich orphan. A little farther on, in the hills, there was a notary. A notary, a cistern, these are things to make use of. First they made Augusta sign a legal notice. Normal. I see Rodolphe. He must have pulled off his hat and scratched his head, then squeezed his chin and pulled two or three times on the skin of his chin. At that point, he said:

"Let us see it."

They passed the paper across the table to him.

He asked several times:

"What does that mean?"

The notary took back the paper, put on his glasses, and reread the act up until the word that Rodolphe kept his finger on.

"There."

"There, that means..."

"Good. It is standard."

Augusta signed, the notary signed. All that was left was to prepare his big hands and the rope.

I read that in Paris certain gun brokers sell revolvers to excited people and, distrusting them, give them blank cartridges. The evil is that in the middle of the land one cannot accomplish acts with blanks.

For Rodolphe, his son, and for the entire chestnut farm, we could perhaps avenge Augusta because they believed too much that the middle of the land was worth the middle of the sea. But I know other stories, another story that the newspapers do not talk about.

Last summer, in a little mountain village, I was going to smoke my pipe along the ravine with a dear old laughing man, slow, filled with wisdom, in bloom from the eye down to the lips. Towards noon his wife called him with a soft, loving voice and he went in to soup. Walking the flat of the fields at his leisure, one felt that he had a firm foot, long thoughts, a good weight.

I said to him often:

"Father Firmin, we are still going to have good pipes before the time..."

It did not bother him to speak about death. Everything was well-oiled in him. He saw himself at the end of his life with still a good bundle of years.

The wife died. Father Firmin stayed alone in the house. Then his nephew came to live in the house. They had spoken so much about company, they had spoken so much about children, little girls, of good society all cosy around the stove, they had waved good soups under his nose, good stews, fresh tobacco, the good young women fussed so much for the pains of the old man that Firmin went to the notary.

Twenty days later, after twenty mouthfuls of a very bitter truth, Firmin threw himself in the torrent.

The nephew is red-haired and a solid man. He has a lot of blood. He has to eat a lot. They are not plentiful, those little fields of dark grain up there in the high waves of the mountain.

Men lost on rafts, in the middle of the land.

Song of the World

For a very long time I have wanted to write a novel in which you could hear the world sing. In all of today's books they have given, in my opinion, too big a place to small-minded people and they have neglected to make us perceive the breathing of the beautiful inhabitants of the universe. The seeds that are sown in books, they all seem to have been purchased from the same granary. They sow a lot about love in all its forms, and it is a thoroughly bastardized plant, then one or two fistfuls of other seeds and that is all. Besides, all of that is sown into man. I know that we can hardly conceive of a novel without people, because they are part of the world. What is needed is to put man in his place, not to make him the center of everything, to be humble enough to perceive that a mountain exists not merely as height and width but as weight, emissions, gestures, overarching power, words, sympathy. A river is a character, with its rages and its loves, its power, its god of chance, its sicknesses, its thirst for adventures. Rivers, springs are characters: they love, they deceive, they lie, they betray, they are beautiful, they dress themselves in rushes and mosses. The forests breathe. The fields, the moors, the hills, the beaches, the oceans, the valleys in the mountains, the lost summits struck by lightning and the proud walls of rock on which the wind of the heights comes to disembowel itself since the first ages of the world: all of this is not a simple spectacle for our eyes. It is a society of living beings. We only know the anatomy of these beautiful living things, as human as we are, and if the mysteries limit us on all sides it is because we have never taken into account the earthly, vegetable, fluvial, and marine psychologies.

This appeasement which comes to us in the friendship of a mountain, this appetite for the forests, this drunkenness which equalizes us, extinguishes our gaze and deadens thought, because we have smelled the odor of these humid burdocks, the mushrooms, the barks, this joy of entering in the grass up to our waist, they are not creations of our senses, it exists all around us and it directs our gestures more than what we believe.

I know that, at times, they have made use of a river to carry the weight of a novel; the silt of its terror, mystery, or strength. I know that they have made use of mountains and that every day they still make use of the land and the fields. They make the birds sing in the forests. No, what I want to do, is to put everything in its place. Despite everything, in the admirable, most recent novel of Jules Romains, Paris is too small. Paris by way of a character is much stronger than that. I know it poorly; the few times that I was there, it showed me the play of some of its muscles so well, the few strokes of its secret battles succeeded so well that ever since I have kept a distant respect for it. In this society of fat inhabitants of the universe, it is, along with all the big cities, the beautiful, cultivated, sportive, seductive, and rotten hoodlum.

If I say that it is small, in this book, it is because for the moment men are too important in relation to it. Besides, it is possible that in the coming volumes, his portrait will be complete and at the end of things we will see Paris as it is: flat, gnawing, scolding, destroyer of the earth, embued with the stinking of human sweat like a great ant hive that exhales its acid.

Yes, they have made use of all that. One should not make use of it. One must see it. One must, I believe, see, love, comprehend, hate the association of men, the world around it, as one is forced to look, to love, to detest men profoundly in order to paint them. One should stop isolating the character-man, sow him with simple, habitual seeds, but show him as he is, that is to say pierced, drunk, weighty and luminous with humors, influences, the song of the world. For whoever has lived a while in a little mountain hamlet, for example, it is useless to say what place that mountain holds in the conversations of men. For a village of fishermen, it is the sea; for a village in the countryside, it is the fields, the wheat, and the prairies. We do not want to isolate man. He is no longer isolated. The face of the earth is in his heart.

To write this novel, all that is needed is new eyes, new ears, new skins, a man bruised enough, beaten enough, flayed enough by life to no longer desire anything but the lullaby sung by the world.

JEAN GIONO (1895–1970) was born in Manosque, Provence, the son of a shoemaker and a washerwoman. A widely loved figure in his native France, he is the author of many books, the best known of which, perhaps, are *Song of the World* and *Horseman on the Roof.* In 1953, he was awarded the Prize of the Prince Rainier de Monaco for his body of work, became a member of the Académie Goncourt in 1954, and accepted a seat on the Literary Counsel of Monaco in 1963.

Except for a few journeys to Paris or abroad, Giono spent his entire life in Manosque, faithful to his native Provence.

HENRY MILLER (1891–1980) is the author of many books, including the classics *Tropic of Cancer* and *Tropic of Capricorn*, which chronicle his life as an American expatriate living in Paris.

EDWARD FORD, a lifelong admirer of Giono's, completed a Master's in French at the University of Virginia. *Solitude de la pitié* was the first book of Giono's he read, and it remains his favorite to this day. Ford lives in the Boston area.